GHOST STORIES

Ghost Stories

———

E. M. BRONER

GLOBAL CITY PRESS

NEW YORK

PERMISSION GRANTED
TO REPRINT THE FOLLOWING:

"Joking Around," *Ascent*;

"My Mother's Madness," in another version, *Ms. Magazine*;

"Carefree Hours," *Frontiers*;

"Song," in another version, *North American Review*;

"Ghost Stories," in altered version *Tikkun*;

"Cousins," in another version, *Voices International* for
National Public Radio;

"My Mother, the Movie Star," *Epoch , vol. 43, no. 1,* and,
in another version, "The Women, the Bitches" in
The Movie That Changed My Life,
ed. David Rosenberg, Viking Penguin;

"Whispering," in another version, *Voices International* for
National Public Radio, and *Heresies*;

"Fat and Fed Up," *13th Moon*.

ISBN 0-9641292-1-3

BOOKS BY E. M. BRONER

FICTION

Ghost Stories

A Weave of Women

Her Mothers

Journal/Nocturnal and Seven Stories

DRAMA

Summer is a Foreign Land

NON-FICTION

The Women's Haggadah (with Naomi Nimrod)

The Telling

The Lost Tradition: Mothers and Daughters in Literature,
editor with Cathy N. Davidson

CONTENTS

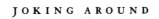

JOKING AROUND

IT'S ONLY LATELY THAT I'VE LOST MY APPETITE. Also eighty pounds. I am suddenly a small person. My voice has changed timbre, going from husky to hoarse.

When Tom left, at a trim 110, he took my weight and my laughter. Upon his departure, all the punchlines evaporated.

Nothing memorable about his wit. Cornball was his style with the classic "Ikey and Mikey" joke or his summer time, "I scream, you scream, we all scream for ice cream."

"How about this twist, kids?" he would say. "My nose is running and my feet are smelling."

I learned to appreciate a joke where a shaggy dog wags its tail from a long ways off. What I can't stand is a joke coming at you a hundred miles an hour and zipping by if you forget to flag it down. Also, I don't appreciate snickering or hateful.

Most of all, I hate the surprise ending, like the O'Henry stories. Like the day Tom died.

Tom had trouble sleeping, the result of a bad cold, maybe a touch of bronchitis.

"How do you feel, dear?" I asked.

"Not very well," he said, the closest I heard him come to complaining.

"What can I do for you, my dear?"

I thought he was answering in a whisper, but he was exhaling his last.

Dying is no joke.

Ever see somebody sitting alone in a movie theater, surrounded by empty chairs, laughing his head off? Or people walking down the street laughing themselves silly?

Phil Donahue says something. I turn to repeat it. It's just an empty arm chair next to me.

I meet a neighbor shopping and try to be social.

"Mrs. Applefeld, did you see Johnny Carson?"

"I don't like boyish-goyish," says Mrs. Applefeld, who tells you more than you ask for.

You have to put on a show for the folks in this retirement community, whose chief crop is fertilizing the ground with its membership. You nod and smile when you encounter a fellow resident. Nobody wears widow's weeds, and, when you speak, it's not to complain.

"So what did Johnny Carson say?" Mrs. Applefeld asks. "How did it go?"

I can't remember. With me nothing goes.

To keep on the safe side, I've stopped laughing.

When I look out the window, I hope for rain.

Tom departed travelling light. The window-dressers of the mortuary chose his dark blue suit, his white shirt still in gift-wrapping. I thought of French cuffs and silver cufflinks, but rejected that as too wasteful. They pulled clean boxer shorts on him and nice navy socks without the tight elastic band that he always hated. They dissuaded me from shoes. It interfered with the smooth line of the layout.

As for the rest of the wardrobe, Salvation Army has become snippity about pick-ups from our retirement community. They could fill their bins on our discards and departures.

"Take something," I tell our son, "a vest, a hanky."

He looks at a box of unused linen handkerchiefs.

"Not my size," he says.

Tom is an angel size.

If I fall asleep, a rarity these days, I feel a tickle. He's turned into a pillow feather. I almost swallow him.

He was always a mannequin, a miniature. He used to sing to me: "Some day she'll come along/the girl I love/and she'll be big and strong/the girl I love." And I did outweigh, outpunch, outlive him. But he took care of me, and now he's not even here to warn me against my new enemies.

A thud against my patio door. I report these early morning thuds to my children.

"It's the newsboys," they tell me.

Only one thing wrong with that reason, there's no paper. I stopped delivery. Who needs the news, births, deaths, crashes in bad weather? I have enough news in me for a lifetime.

In the meantime, my across-the-street neighbor pulls her drapes aside to spy on me. She wants to know where my stocks and bonds are hidden.

I report this to the children.

"What does your neighbor look like?" they test me.

"Like a neighbor," I reply.

My daughters and son sit on the couch looking out the window facing her apartment.

"Nobody's looking," they report after about a minute-and-a-half.

As soon as the kids drive off, my neighbor sashes up her drape. Beady eyes peek out. We're not allowed animals in this compound, but a weasel's snuck in.

Out of honor to Tom's habits, I turn on Dan Rather.

"She's abreast of the news," Tom used to say, copping a feel of my 42s.

He was not a mechanical man. I would have to extricate him from my brassiere when his hand developed a cramp.

"Dan," I would say, blacking out the TV, "you're no substitute."

The world has become too bright, too much sun or street light. I close my eyes. Light bulbs burst against the lids.

The children come over.

"Mom, look at me."

I shadow my eyes with my hand.

"It's too bright," I say.

"Do you know who I am?" one or the other asks.

Children aren't as important as they think they are.

"It's you," I say, "the pesky one."

"I've made an appointment for you at the doctor's," says my concerned eldest.

"He'll say, 'mumbo jumbo,' and hold out his hand for my money," I tell her.

"First we'll have a nice lunch," says my youngest, "then drop in for a check-up."

"What kind of doctor?" I ask.

I'm suddenly aware of the corn on my little toe.

"I could see a podiatrist," I agree.

Even though I am out there in the dark, under an awning of hand, I can feel them exchange glances.

"If that's what you want," says my son, a conciliatory fellow.

With eyes closed, I grope, select some dress, button it down evenly or crookedly. To top off the outfit, I wear red-rimmed sunglasses.

"It's an overcast day," says my responsible eldest daughter. "You don't need sunglasses."

She gently tries to lift them off my eyes. I hang onto the ear pieces.

"Wear them if you need them," she gives in.

At lunch I order salad but soon set down the fork. Everything chopped tastes the same whether potatoes or tomatoes, cucumbers or pears.

"Time for an appointment," says my son, the middle child, always time-keeper, whistle-blower, referee.

We're at the office.

My daughters each take an arm. I dig in my heels and pull back.

7

"Help! Help!" I appeal to a passing stranger. "They're leading me to my slaughter."

"Mother!" says my eldest.

"You're lying about the podiatrist," I say. "It's a psychiatrist. You want to prove me nuts so you can get at my stocks and bonds."

"Not true!" says my youngest.

"Stop that sniveling," I say. "You two are always bawling or bullying."

Soon as I enter the office I know she's a phony. First, her little head barely reaches the back of her little chair. Second, she has the expression a prune. I know from recent history that the only thing prunes are good for is constipation.

"Do you know what day it is?" she asks, lifting her pencil to take notes on my brilliant reply.

"Of course."

She waits. "What day?"

"None of your business."

"Do you know who is President of the United States?"

"The wrong man," I tell her.

This had been the case since FDR died.

When they get me back in the car, I take off my sunglasses and look at them good.

"You damned hypocrites," I say.

I'll never close my eyes again. The enemy is advancing. Who knows where they'll put me if my guard is down?

Even with my eyes wide-open I can't protect

myself. My bowels stop functioning. I become an old storage bin. My belly is hard and gassy. When the kids visit, first thing, they open doors and windows, and flap their hands.

"Dying is easy," I once told Tom. "It's sick I'm afraid of."

"I'm afraid of your going before me," says my husband. "Promise you won't."

"How can I promise?" I ask. "You know I've got anemia, angina, a bad kidney. You're hardy as a horse. You'll get on a new wife and gallop off."

He takes my left hand, the one on which he put the wedding band when the hand was a girl's. I see how deeply the ring has bitten into the finger, how swollen the knuckles are.

"Promise," he says.

"I promise," I vow.

Sixty years ago I promised to love him. A year ago I promised to outlive him.

I've cursed myself for not breaking that last promise.

"You coward!" I cry. "Selfish! Even leaving me your dirty underwear to launder."

To whom am I complaining? The twin armchair before the TV? The dining room chair at the head of the table?

"I envy you your eyes and ears," Tom used to tell me.

"I don't blame you," I said. "Twenty/twenty vision and I can hear a pin drop."

Tom's worn glasses since childhood, making him

look studious even before he could read. His hearing has been going for a while. He'd be vague during family dinners and the kids began to worry that he was out of it. To be in it, he ordered a new double hearing aid. Just before it arrived, he departed. There's the set, waiting to eavesdrop on family dinners, sitting in his drawer. I've let them bill me over and over for it. That's one bill I haven't the heart to pay.

Tom, his face like waxed fruit, his ears waxed over, couldn't hear me if I sang along with a symphony.

Tom couldn't hear but my neighbors did. Mrs. Applebaum, to whom I made the mistake of entrusting my eldest daughter's phone number, called about screaming coming from my house.

Before I know it, I'm on the other side of the doctor's desk.

"Do you remember me?" she asks. "Who am I?"

"I met you once before," I say.

She nods.

"In the movie *The Wizard of Oz*," I tell her. "You played a munchkin."

"Mother!" says my youngest.

"You were a psychologist," I correct myself, "to the Wizard of Oz."

"Psychiatrist! I'm a psychiatrist!" she tells me. Then she lowers her voice. "Are you feeling hostile to me?"

"Pish posh," I say to her.

She writes a prescription and bill that will cut nicely into my survivor's pension, thank you. She doesn't hand the Rx to me but to my eldest.

"She wants to dope me up," I say, "so she can get at my stocks and bonds."

It's M & M time, morning and evening, red for stool softener, blue for heart, yellow to make me mellow.

Every couple of days I see one or all of the children. If they're expecting to freeload a meal, they won't get it from me. Especially if they're company spies, reporting back to Doctor Munchkin.

When the family leaves, the drapes across the road flutter.

I tell my son, "It's worse now. She's not alone. Her nephew is fixing his sights on me."

My son looks doubtful.

"I have proof," I say. "He's practicing with a slingshot or B B gun. Pellets are hitting the window of my bedroom."

"It could be a branch, Mom," says my son, trying for reason.

"Could be but isn't," I say. "Who are you believing, me or a stranger?"

"Have you met her nephew?" asks my son, the referee.

"Don't be silly! You think she would make a formal introduction if he's planning a sneak attack?"

"You're sure she has a nephew living with her?" asks my eldest, the truth-seeker.

"Why don't you ask me the day of the week and the President of the USA?" I say.

My youngest visits.

"The bed is stretching," I show her. "It's getting bigger. I roll all over it, like aboard a ship in a storm."

"It's all the weight you've lost, Mama," she says. "Let's go for munchies."

She persuades me to eat dessert—pie a la mode, with a ginger ale drink.

I come home, close the door, and the world is as it was an hour before.

Why eat when there's no partner?

Why keep abreast, when there's only the past?

Once in a while I try my old tv buddy, Phil Donahue. The audience is shrieking. The camera shows ugly people, mouths open, roaring at my condition.

"It's no laughing matter," I tell them.

"It's dark as pitch in here," says my eldest, lighting every lamp as if I'm John D. Rockefeller.

She snaps the shades so old nosy can look in unimpeded.

"Are you taking your pill," my youngest asks, "the one the psychiatrist prescribed?"

"That's a bitter pillow to swallow," I joke.

"What does it do, Mama?" my eldest asks.

"It doesn't do anything. That's why I'm not taking it anymore."

MIS-TAKE.

"You haven't put on your clothes in a week," says the son, promoted to chief of police.

"I'm more comfortable this way."

"How do you get to the laundry room like that?" he asks, still trying to solve the case.

"I don't dirty anything," I explain.

I can see that I gave all the wrong answers. They're

going to flunk me out of this house to the place we old ones dread.

"Shoot me," says Mrs. Applebaum, "if my children want to put me in a nursing home."

I outsmart them. I dress and button with eyes open. I invite them for dinner. I do the laundry and pile it so the kids can count sheets, towels and pillow cases. I leave the drapes open, the shades up even at night. In their presence I do not mention my neighbor.

"Phil told a good one today," I say laughing.

They look at one another across the table smiling.

"What did he say, Mom?" asks my biggest girl.

"He said," my thoughts jumble. I grab at a familiar one floating by. "He said,

'There was an old woman
who lived in a shoe
she had so many children
she didn't know what to do.'

That's you," I grin at them.

My son puts down his fork. "Donahue said that?"

"I'm just kidding," I say. "Here's one."

I grab my baby girl's arm:

"'Hickory Dickory Dock
The mouse ran up the clock.'"

I tickle her up and down the arm like I used to do. She doesn't tickle.

"Can't you people take a joke?" I ask. "Here's your last chance. Mary, the Virgin, is visited by the Angel. He has an announcement to make. Mary will give birth to a baby, a son, who will be the son of God.

"'Gee,' says Mary, 'I wanted a girl.'"

"That's good, Mother," says my eldest, patting me.

As they leave I tell them politely, "Thank you. Come again."

I read that somewhere.

I lie down in my clothes, not to have to go through all this dressing and undressing.

The nephew sends spitballs against my window. Under me the mattress heaves. My head rolls from pillow to pillow. A feather floats out of the pillow and up my nose. I sneeze.

"God bless!" says Tom, slowing the bobbing bed, his head stilling my heart.

"Tom?"

"The Piper's son," he says, jaunty as ever.

"Was that you watching from across the road?"

"Peeping Tom," says Old Cornball.

"Tom," I say, "you took your time about it."

"I sent signals against the window."

He looks at me stretched out.

"Not much body left to you. You're taking employment away from the scarecrows."

"Tom," I say, "I have a joke for you. I went to a podiatrist and she turned out to be a psychiatrist. She said, 'There's something terribly wrong with you. Your nose is running and your feet are smelling.'"

"Leave them laughing, kiddo," says Tom.

And we do.

MY MOTHER'S MADNESS

IN MY MOTHER'S MEMOIRS, I HAVE THREE mentions: birth, marriage and children. My younger brother fared better: also playing the trumpet in the district school band, and medical school.

There were more notable events to supercede us in the memoir: her two years in private school where she wore a uniform of green wool with white starched apron, and learned French; the pogroms, the outbreak of typhus that took her eldest brother and father in the same week; hearing and cheering Trotsky; emigration; the hard wait in Poland for her visa; the harder years in the Midwest working in the laundry; the English classes at night school; the marriage proposal.

"What do you want to do more than anything?" her love had asked her.

"I want to read all the books in the library," she replied.

"So be it," he promised.

Except for a brief period during her marriage, she did

not work, but, in every town or city in which he worked, they were within walking distance of the library.

"What if I finish all the books?" she asked her husband.

"We'll move," said my father.

Their last move was to a West Coast retirement village where the library was located in a bank since more people deposited money than withdrew books.

"Our marriage was like a Great Books Club," said my mother. "We read. We discussed."

Now she turns the pages silently.

My mother outlived my father by two years and her memoir by a decade and, during those years, there was affection between us.

In her memoir she gave everybody's name and name change, the Americanization of the names, maiden name turned to married name, nickname to formal name.

She named me *Leila*, Hebrew and Arabic for *night*.

"It was a dark time for me," she wrote in the memoir, "when night fell on my learning."

Yet, in her last decade, as I flew from the East Coast to the West, I gained more than the three hours' time difference.

She waited at the gate of her patio for the airport limousine.

"Leila," she said as I descended, "you made my day."

I have not had enough of this. I could get used to it, but I don't have the chance.

My mother sits cranked up in her hospital bed.

"Leila," she says, "I'm going down the hill."

"Downhill," I say automatically.

"Thank you," says my mother. "I appreciate correction of my English."

The next moment her eyes unfocus. Each looks in a different direction.

"Leila, they're on my roof!"

She clutches the bedsheet.

"Who, Mama?"

"The Cossacks!"

"The Cossacks were disbanded," I say.

I imagine this is true.

My mother comes to herself.

"Thank you," she says. "I like history to be accurate."

My mother is in her world of seventy years ago.

"They're stealing my goods," says mother the next day when I visit her in the hospital.

"Who, Mother?"

"The *muziks*," she says.

"There are no *muziks* in the hospital," I tell her, "only Muzak."

My mother does not appreciate this information.

"The daughter contradicts the mother," she says. "What kind of world is this?"

"She has received an insult," my doctor brother explains out of my mother's hearing.

"Who insulted her?" I ask.

"Her body," says my brother. "She had an embolism in the kidneys that affected the mind."

We re-enter the room.

"Go to the banks," mother tells my brother.

"Which bank?" he asks.

"Where I have my accounts," she says. "They're stealing interest from me."

"I'll go," my brother says. "I'll take care of it."

"Hurry up, damn you," says our mother. "I haven't got all day."

"I'm going, Mother," says my brother, "on my day off."

My mother shakes her finger at her son.

"My Fancy Pants. Mr Big Shot. The Doctor to the World will find the time for his mother."

My brother, in turn, shakes his finger at her.

"Don't you shake a finger at me," he says. "I dismissed my patients to be with you."

"Dock me," says my mother.

"Take it easy," says her son.

"While the Nazi steals from me, while the Arab steals from me, I should take it easy?"

"What Nazi? What Arab?" I ask my brother.

"That's what she calls the bank tellers," he says. "The blonde woman is a Nazi. The brunette is an Arab."

"That's right," agrees my mother. "And look in the safety deposit box. They'd love to get their hands on my valuables and liquidate me."

"What valuables?" I ask my brother.

"Her citizenship papers," he tells me, "her passport photo."

"Everything is for you," says mother, "the two of you."

She begins to cry. I've heard her cry only once

before, when my father died. It sounds forced, unnatural. She's not used to shedding tears.

"Why do you think I didn't buy a dress, hire a maid, go on holiday?" asks my mother.

"You bought a dress," says my brother. "You've had a maid. You could have gone on holiday."

"You don't understand anything," says my mother. "What I spend I take from the mouths of my children and grandchildren."

"Your children are middle-aged," I tell her. "Your grandchildren are all grown up and can get their own food."

My mother snorts. Her husband did not get his own food but had his place set for him, his meal served to him.

One day, two years ago, after his usual breakfast of poached eggs on whole wheat, a lunch of toasted cheese sandwich, a dinner of boiled chicken without the skin, spiced with garlic power and paprika, my father died.

Soon after, my mother began to fear intruders.

"The Cossacks are riding on my roof," she phoned me on the East Coast.

"What time is it?" asks Samuel.

"3:00 AM," I tell him. "Mother," I say, "the roof isn't strong enough to hold horse and rider."

She's phoned again, this time at dawn. Samuel's eyes open wide. Mine are still closed.

"They're peering through the windows," says my mother.

I hang up and call my brother. It's 3:00 AM in California.

"What time is it?" he asks. "I just fell asleep. I had a late emergency operation." He bestirs himself. "Nobody can peer through her windows," he assures me, if not our mother, "because she's ordered double drapes and blinds. The place is like wartime black-out."

The next time she phones, at noon, I say, "Mother, it isn't so."

"Woe is me when the child turns a deaf ear to the adult."

I'm impressed.

"Nicely expressed," I say.

"Thank you," she says politely. "I do like a nice turn of phrase."

Her illness has a name.

"Uremic poisoning," says the urologist my brother has consulted.

The insulted kidneys in turn have insulted the brain.

"Let's give dialysis a chance," says the urologist.

"He's only a fortune teller," says my mother about the urologist.

"He predicts that you'll get better," says my brother.

My mother neatly packs an overnight bag with brush, comb, lipstick, a change of underwear, robe and slippers.

She is attached to the dialysis machine.

"Lie still," says the dialysis nurse, "and our blood will be washed clean and the poison removed."

"You have dirty blood too?" asks my mother.

I phone from New York.

"Do you feel better, Mother?" I ask.

"Ask the fortune teller," she says. "For me, a minute is like an hour, an hour is forever."

"Beautifully expressed," I compliment her.

"I try to be descriptive," says my mother.

My brother phones me from Orange County to New York. His voice is higher pitched as he relates the conversation with our mother.

"She said, 'I can't stay here any more because the aides steal from me.'

"'What can they possibly steal, Mother?'

"'My glasses. These are the wrong glasses. The Black nurse, he took mine.'

"'He didn't need your glasses, Mother. He has his own.'

"'He also stole my book,' she said.

"'What book? That's his pharmacy book.'

"'All books belong to me,' said our mother."

When I speak to her again long-distance, she says, "I can't read. That's the saddest thing of all in my life."

"She needs a cataract operation, but I'm afraid," my brother calls me back to explain.

The enemy is peering through every aperture, clogging them.

"They won't let me move my bowels," she phones from her room. "They hold it in."

My brother sighs and phones back that he has prescribed stool softener, laxative, enemas.

"She only talks about shit to me," he says.

My mother leaves the hospital for home.

She phones at any hour of the day or night. My mother never sleeps.

"She's mad," I tell Samuel.

"They steal from me at the supermarket," says my mother. "They print one price right over the other. It's become a nation of thieves."

"That's not madness," says Samuel.

She eats less and less in order not to fill the coffers of the thieves.

The next call my mother begins by swearing.

"Ah *chalariah*," that dreaded curse, May cholera fall upon you! "My medicine is breaking me. The cost is tripling. They take advantage of the weak, the elderly and the sick."

"Well put," I say.

She hangs up pleased.

This is also not madness.

My brother calls me, from his Coast to mine. He is encouraged.

"She borrowed a sewing machine from one of her neighbors," says my brother. "She wants to take in all her dresses. It's something to do since she lost all the weight from not eating."

His optimism is short-lived. He phones again the next night.

"She's not sewing. She's sitting shredding all of her dresses," he says.

I fly out to my mother and brother.

On the screen is a made-for-airplane film, ignored by crew and passengers. Cars race, the police shoot, but window shades are up, reading lights are on and the passengers stroll the aisle.

Mother is back in the hospital. I read her *Los Angeles Times* while she dozes.

When she awakens, I tell her the news.

"Like you, Mother," I say, "Barbara Bush has also been hospitalized."

"And I bet she's tired of lying around," says my mother.

"Would you like to take a walk?" I ask, offering her an arm.

She nods, leaning on me. We walk the corridors slowly. She looks curiously into each room. In one, flowers abound.

Suddenly she darts away, into that patient's room.

"Look at all the flowers!" she says. "You must be Barbara Bush."

Mother is refusing her sedatives and her other pills on the basis of color.

"I don't like dark blue," she says. "That doesn't look good on me."

"Mother," says my brother, "that's your heart medicine."

She's given sedation by injection and, at last, dozes. My brother and I each hold one of her hands. We study her face for evidence, for explanation. Only our holding so tightly onto her keeps her here.

There is an emergency. The urologist tells my brother that the hospital can no longer keep our mother.

"She's not sick," he says. "She's dying. And that could take a while."

"So, the fortune teller washes his hands of me," says my mother.

I fly out again.

Nurses and aides have tied my mother to her bed until my brother makes other arrangements for her. She's been agitated and violent. She bit one aide and scratched another.

"They deserved it," says my mother. "They took my eyes."

Mother turns to my brother.

"Do you still have your swimming pool?" she asks.

"Where else would my pool go?" says my brother.

"Then bring me my bathing suit," says my mother.

"You want to go swimming, Mother? You haven't been in a pool for years."

"Yes," says my mother. "Take me to your house. Get me my bathing suit. I have to commit suicide."

We're corridor-consultants, my brother and I.

"It's clear we can't take her to my place," says my brother.

We settle upon House of Care.

"Is it a beauty parlor?" our mother asks.

My brother drives us there. The stucco is a bright pink.

"It's the right color," says my mother. "It matches my bathrobe and slippers."

"Will you be happy here, Mother?" I ask.

She looks around. "I have an announcement to make. I'm going home."

"But the Cossacks are there," I say.

"And the *muziks*," says my brother.

"You've got to be kidding," she says.

Her nice room is prepared for her arrival with a bouquet of flowers on her dresser.

"What's this going to run me?" asks our mother. "The room, the care, and, wait, they'll double-bill me for the flowers."

"Medicare," lies my brother. "They're paying it."

"Three thousand a month," he had told me. "All her hard-earned savings."

"Another announcement," says my mother. "I've decided I want my freedom. Freedom now!"

"That's already been said, Mother," I remind her.

"All right," says mother. "I don't like to take words from the mouths of others."

"Make yourself at home," says a pleasant aide.

"I can't," says my mother, "simply because this is not my home. My home is patiently waiting for my return."

"Mother!" says my brother.

She shakes her finger. He shakes his finger.

"I shake my finger at my son and he shakes his finger at me, and we stand here until our fingers cross like swords," says mother.

"You do have a way with words," I tell her.

"I worked at it," says she.

The next day I visit her at House of Care.

"Rose called," she says. "Remember my neighbor Rose?"

A peppy small woman who still drives at eighty.

"How is Rose?"

"Aside from her cataracts, her deafness and the arthritis that makes claws of her hands, Rose is doing just fine."

I hesitate.

"Mother," I say.

"What is it, Leila? I haven't got all day."

I want to tell her that we've put a deposit on a shared house in Italy. I want to tell her that we purchased our tickets before she became so ill.

"I bought airplane tickets to Italy."

She's quiet.

"The thieves," says my mother. "Since decontrol, they've got a monopoly. They don't let you return a ticket."

Sane again.

"You hit the nail on the head, Mother," I say.

"Cliche," she tells me.

"Sorry."

"As for me," says mother, "I'm sitting here only day by day. We don't know what's written on the calendar."

My brother has said much the same, only not so well.

"So, go with Samuel and your friends," says mother. "Leila by day, Leila by night, Leila, my delight."

"Lovely," I say.

"It should be," she tells me. "Who wrote the memoir?"

We hold hands, then she disentangles hers.

"One thing," she says. "When I go, bind the memoir and send it to the library at the bank."

In my brother's house, in my house, in our children's houses, it will bind our history.

CAREFREE HOURS

IN ORANGE COUNTY THERE IS A ROAD THAT takes care of automobile, animal and human: the Golden Valley Auto Body Shop, Golden Valley Animal Hospital, followed by the human Hospital, the Los Caballeros Sports Center to build up the body, and Carefree Hours Nursing Home after the body can no longer be built up.

Carefree Hours is peach stucco with orange tile and green shutters. Its staff is Chicana, Chicano; the supervisory staff is Caucasian. The patients are mostly WASPS with one or two well-off Asians. What distinguishes the patients is their mode of transportation: cane, walker, wheelchair.

At lunch, a tall pale man, wearing a cap, tries to bring the chicken croquette to his mouth. His hand shakes the croquette off the fork. Despite palsy, he tries again, until someone else's wheelchair knocks against his arm. The croquette is determinedly gathered, piled, approaches his mouth when adjoining

tablemates settle in and dislodge the contents of the
fork. The third time the diner is distracted and misses
his mouth.

He is not being noticed. Who among the serving staff
could pay him any mind with an imperious woman in a
wheelchair tapping her spoon against her glass?

"Cranberry juice!" she calls out, over and over.

Her robe is striped like a Pharaoh's.

"I have to teach them their job," she says to her table
partners. "Since I came here six months ago, there isn't
one person the same working at this place."

But then there aren't that many patients who are
here more than six months.

One of the diners of the neighboring table speaks.
She is the historian of her life here, as she was the historian of her Methodist church back East.

"We're having our sesquicentennial," she says.

The woman is recovering from surgery after being
rear-ended.

My mother sits at a table with me as her luncheon
guest. She grins in triumph for she has been served not
only cranberry juice but two glasses.

"The other glass is mine!" calls out the Pharaoh.

"My daughter's," says my mother and pushes the
juice at me, whispering, "Drink fast."

"You can *will* yourself to separate from pain," says
the church historian. "You can rise above it. I won't
take their pain pills. I would rather pace the floor."

"I don't agree with you," says the Pharaoh. "Pain is
unnatural and should be sedated."

It is an interesting dispute. My mother, however, does not socialize or enter into such discussions. When she is wheeled down to meals, she always asks to sit alone.

"Why do you want to come down here?" asks the aide, who had dressed her, combed her, put on her make-up.

"Because you make me," says my mother ungraciously.

"I'll give you an example," lectures the historian. "I have head pains, fist-clenching head pains. A wow of pain! But I won't give in to it. I'll conquer and return to my post at the church."

"Hotsy totsy," says my mother about the table of the Pharaoh and the historian. "Not so hotsy totsy," she says, regarding cottage cheese and mayonnaisey tuna.

She is returned to her room.

"*Oi!*" says Mama.

In Carefree Hours, nobody *Oi*s.

"*Oi, veh's mir*," says my mama, rubbing her bloated belly.

Her belly swells the covers. She is also breathing with difficulty. Her room is cold because of the oxygen tank. The little rubber tube encircles her head, releases oxygen into her nostrils.

"Mama!" cries my mother. "Mama, Mama. Help me!"

But her mama isn't here.

"*I'm* here," I say.

"Don't you go leaning on me," she says.

She had given birth to my brother in her forties and

never let out a moan. She is proud of this information in her life's resume.

"I'm older than the other women," she said in the labor room, "and I have to set an example."

Now they are all the same age.

"Ai yi," says my mother.

Music comes in through the windows. It is a marimba band whose music wafts down the avenue from Los Caballeros Sports Center. They are playing *Dolores*, "Ay yi, Dolores, Ay yi/ai yi/lala la…"

It's a duet, outside and inside Carefree Hours.

"I can't stand it!" says my mother.

"The pain?"

"The band."

The aides have put restraints on my mother. At first I think it is a kind of bolero like the marimba players wear. But hers was tied to the wheelchair to keep her from sliding down and now it is fastened to the railings of the bed.

I close the window and Mama sings her own song:

Oi, Mama, what am I going to do?
I can't stand it anymore.
I can't stand it anymore.
What will become of me?

A tall, dignified woman wheels by, looking in sympathetically.

"Tell Eleanor Roosevelt to mind her own business," my mother calls.

Mother is not alone in the room. Her roommate is a Japanese woman, quiet and uncomplaining.

The Japanese woman's daughter visits daily. The son is there every evening. The handsome grandson comes about dinnertime and brings his grandmother little presents on each visit, a mirror, a flower, a comb. The family talcum powders their mother's sores; they turn her gently; they bring Japanese food to whet her appetite.

"Speak to her, Mama," I have encouraged.

"She doesn't speak," says my mother.

The roommate, however, has picked up a few English expressions.

"Take it easy," the roommate calls to me when visiting hours are over.

Now and then I hear an exhalation of breath or a sharp pant from her.

"Riddled with cancer," says her son, wetting a washcloth and wiping her face.

"She's so nice," I tell my mother.

"Miles apart," says mother. "Can't you see, we're miles apart?"

On this day, my mother's eyes are closed. She has not looked at me this evening's visit. She opens her eyes a slit.

"Honey," she says.

"Yes, Mama."

"Help me."

Oh, would we all if we could, the family of the Japanese matron; Eleanor Roosevelt's schoolteacher daughter, even the descendants of the impatient woman in her striped robe.

I search for the RN on the floor.

"I have others to help," she tells me sternly. "Her turn will come."

I return to the room. My mother's stomach hurts. She rubs it over and over. An hour passes. Another hour. I stop her hand by placing mine over hers; she knocks my hand off.

The daughter of the Japanese patient regards us.

"She raised you," says the daughter, "and now you have the honor of caring for her."

The roommate's family selects a station and leaves the TV on when they depart. Their ninety-four-year-old mother is being acculturated into the 1950s, the '60s. All the sit-coms appear on this particular channel. *The Partridge Family* is playing, with blonde Miss Susan Dey, who spent the last thirty years in our living room growing up.

My mother opens her mouth wide to moan. Her teeth have been hacked away by a dentist who does not care how his elderly patients look. Until recently, Mama kept a full mouth of healthy, widely-spaced teeth.

"A symphony of teeth," a dentist of her past used to say admiringly.

On TV, Gidget falls in love. There is young Sally Fields.

The nurse takes my mother's blood sugar.

"It's high," she says. "I'll have to phone her doctor."

"But the stomach ache?" I ask.

"I can't deal with everything at once," says the nurse.

On the TV, Fred Gwynne is playing a Munster.

I leave for the night, not able to offer help to anyone, not my mother rubbing her belly, not her panting roommate, not Gidget and her romance or the Munsters in their turmoil.

The next day I walk past the mall with the pharmacy, Anita's Hamburgers, Senor Reubin's Tacos, those hospitals for autos, humans and pets and, last of all, to colorful Carefree Hours.

Mother's bed is empty.

Is she dead?

"She's in the Lounge," says the same RN from last night.

"She's feeling better?" I ask.

"She must be," says the nurse. "She was all dolled up."

She's not in the Lounge.

"There's another lounge, other side of the floor," says an aide.

Mother is not there. My mother's been kidnapped or has flown the coop.

Someone else greets me. I almost don't recognize Mother in the crimson robe with the green paisley pattern. Her eyes, shut all evening, are open this afternoon, magnified by her bifocals.

"Hello!" she says delightedly. "Do come to lunch with me."

"I'm not allowed twice," I say.

"Never mind," says my mother. "We'll *make* them serve you."

It is the same scene as yesterday. I am awkward

with the wheelchair and knock against the table where the palsied gentleman is trying to spoon soup into his mouth.

"Get that woman driver out of here!" he shouts.

The woman in the striped robe says, "You're not allowed to have guests twice in a week for lunch."

"She's jealous," whispers my mother.

Mrs. Roosevelt nods her head at my mother and asks, "How are you today?"

My mother does not answer.

"Answer her, Mama," I say.

"You answer once, they ask again," says my mother.

At her name plate is the wrong meal. A ham sandwich. Mother shrugs.

"So tell me where it isn't anti-Semitic," she says.

"Mistake," I tell the aide. "She's kosher."

"Is baloney kosher?"

I shake my head.

"Is shrimp salad kosher?"

Mother just raises her eyes.

"Cheese sandwich, then. Never heard anything against toasted cheese," says the earnest aide.

"Except cholesterol," says Mrs. Roosevelt.

We split the toasted cheese and cholesterol. My mother drinks her cranberry juice and requests another, looking sideways at the woman in the striped robe to see if she's been served her first glass of juice.

"Let's go out on the patio," I say to Mama.

It's not so easy, even though the patio leads off from the lunchroom. The RN has to unlock the patio door for us. It's kept locked and alarmed or all the Carefree Hours people would wheel, trundle, creep their way out of the home.

The band from Los Caballeros is playing. We can feel the beat under us on the patio. Mama's hair is lifted in the breeze like dandelion fluff. It rises, it settles down. *Dolores* is playing over the wall.

"I went to activities this morning," says my mother.

"Did you? What did you do?"

"We sang."

Her soft voice can still carry a tune.

"*Ai! Ai! Dolores!*"

The present floats in and out.

She dozes and awakens suddenly.

"Hurry," she says. "It's time."

"Time for what, Mother?"

"Take me back," she whispers.

I wheel her back to the air conditioning.

I ask two aides to help me lift her on the bed. It is then that I discover she is wearing diapers and has soiled them.

While I'm waiting in the Visitors' Lounge next door for the change, the RN appears.

"She will never get well," says the RN. "You know that, don't you?"

Who knows such a thing? The woman has misread her job description. She thinks she's the Angel of Death.

"It will be up and down from now on," says the nurse. "Shall I delineate it for you?"

"No," I say, but she does.

"Your mother has lost control of:

1. eyes
2. lungs
3. kidneys
4. bladder
5. bowels
6. heart."

From her room, Mama begins her moaning song.

"We have to remove the gas," says the RN, assigning this messy task to two Chicana women.

"We do a reverse enema on her," they say.

They more than earn their minimum wage.

I hear my mother gasping.

"Be a good girl," says the RN. "Try to control yourself. You don't want to disturb the others."

"What the hell do I care?" asks my mother.

An aide appears in the lounge with mother's soiled sheets and gown in a plastic case.

"The procedure is through," she says.

I go into Mama's room. Her roommate is asleep. *I Love Lucy* is on, all of its major lovable characters dead.

Mother cannot be aroused for a good night.

The next morning, there is my bright-faced mother.

"They all get sundowner's," says an aide. "Every night they lose it and every morning some of them find it again."

"Finders keepers," laughs another aide. "Losers weepers."

"How sweet of you to come," says Mama, patting my cheek as I kneel at her wheelchair.

"I have to go back home, Mama," I say. "I have to fly away today."

She blinks and thinks about this. She has forgotten that I live somewhere else, not in her city, not on this mile-long, pet-to-patient complex.

Mama says, "Turn my chair around to the window."

Her back is to me. I see the straps of the restraining jacket.

Her head tilts up to the sky. The edge of the American flag flutters, planted on the soil of Carefree Hours.

"Take it easy," says my mother, not turning her head.

The roommate presses her remote control and the room slides into the '50s when there was domestic comedy and beach boys swam and the roommates were full of life.

SONG

MY BROTHER PHONES. "SHE IS SETTLING into a coma."

He has visited our mother in the nursing home.

"She has received good care," he says, and tells me about a burly, mustached Chicano worker who tried to coax our mother to eat.

"'Mama,' the hospital worker said, 'Just a little soup, a little Jello?'

"But she doesn't have the strength to sip through a straw," says my brother.

Her body is disobedient to its training and its history. Eyes will not focus; legs refuse to stand; the heart will not do its job. For the past two weeks she has been wearing diapers.

"They want to insert a tube through her nostril into her stomach," says my brother. "I told them, 'Nothing doing!'"

My mother is sinking. We are allowing this to happen.

"Her hands were twitching. She was wringing them," says my brother. "And I sat there and held them for an hour until she crossed them and slept."

Two weeks ago I flew to mother.
Only two weeks ago she could still sing.
I'm at her bedside. She's chilled; her teeth chatter.
"Blankets!" she calls. "More blankets!"
At ninety-eight dollars a day, three thousand a month, she should have an extra blanket.
"Make a fire," she tells me.
"There's no fireplace here, Mama."
"I forget," says my mother.
The fire reminds her of a camp song, one she used to sing at Camp *Mechia*.
"An Indian name?" I ask.
"Yiddish," says mother. "Camp Pleasure.

"Arum dem fayher
mir zinger lider"

"What's that?" I interrupt.
"Around the fire
we're singing songs
the night's so beautiful
one never tires."
"ABCA," I say. "That's the rhyme."
"It rhymes better in Yiddish," says mama. "You know I used to have a good voice."
Today she breathes heavily. Water in her lungs.
The nurse comes to check blood sugar. On top of all her other medical problems, she's newly developed diabetes and has two insulin shots a day.

"How long should we do this to her?" asks my brother when we meet later.

Now my mother turns towards me.

"Campfire days," says Mama drowsily.

*"Arum dem fayer
mir frelekh tantsn."*

"What did you sing, Mama?"

"I was more thinking than singing," says my Mother, "that we, around the fire, were dancing so lively."

I suddenly want to know everything she remembers.

"Take this down," says Mama.

I pick up a notebook I always carry.

"A recipe," says Mama. "What's my best?"

"Stuffed cabbage," I say.

"Olipses," says Mama. "Sit me up. I can't remember when I lie flat. The thoughts run out of the top of the head."

I crank her up. She remembers stuffed cabbage:

"Cook cabbage, not too soft.
Cool
1 LB. meat to head of cabbage
Add salt and pepper to taste
also:
saute 1 large onion
small can mushrooms
raisins."

She pauses, breathing heavily.

An aide pokes her head in.

"Mamacita," she says, "how about a little oxygen for dessert?"

With the tube in her nostrils, Mama continues.

"Did I say salt and pepper? Onion? Raisins? Now, mix together.

"Fold mixture inside cabbage
Add one large can tomatoes
Lemon and sugar to taste
Add water to pot to cover mixture
Cook until meat is done by testing with fork."

She leans back. "Did I say lemon? Did I say sugar?"
I nod.
"So, that's *Olipses*."
I repeat her recipe back to her. She listens and nods her head.
"Now, meat borscht," I say.
"First, tuna salad," she says, "the kind you and your brother loved as children."
"I know how to make tuna salad," I say.
"Who's supposed to talk, and who's supposed to listen?" asks my mother.
"Tuna," she begins,

"Celery
1 hard boiled egg
mayonnaise
sweet pickles.

"That's the trick," says mother, "sweet pickles."
"Nobody eats mayonnaise, Mother," I say. "Cholesterol."
"So eat it dry," says my mother. "It's your funeral."
I pause a moment.
"How about yogurt instead?" I ask.

"How about mayonnaise half and yogurt half, and it's a deal," says my mother.

"Now the meat borscht," I say.

"I'm tired," says Mama. "While I'm on the IV, I don't like to think of food."

She begins to doze on one elbow.

She's sleeping on my visiting time.

"Tell me more, Mama," I say.

"*Sha Sha*," says Mama.

With her eyes closed she sings:

"Sha Shtil!
Macht nischt keyn gerider
Der rebbe gyt shoyn
tantsn vider.

"It means:

"Shh! Be still!
Don't make a sound.
The rabbi's going to
Dance around."

She leans back. "With nothing else working, at least I'm not a *shtimme*, deaf and dumb."

We sit quietly. She begins to sleep. Her mouth drops open. She frowns deeply, then awakens with a start.

"What is it, Mama?"

"I forgot to give you my Russian Beef Borscht. Meat bones. Go to the butcher and get meat bones."

"Nobody goes to the butcher, Mama," I say.

"So don't make meat borscht," she replies.

"OK. Tell me. I'll go."

She draws a breath.

"Meat bones with a little meat attached
potato
raw onion whole
carrots whole
fresh beets
Wash beets, grate them."

"With the leaves?" I ask.

"Some do. I don't," says Mama. "No leaves if you want my meat borscht.

"Salt, pepper, sugar
Can of tomatoes
Cook together."

"Anything else?" I ask.

"If you got lima beans, also add."

"And then?" I ask.

"Then you got borscht."

She wants to slip away into sleep.

"Any more recipes? Any more songs? Did you sing me lullabies?"

"No," said Mother. "In Russia, lullabies were too sad. All about a widow singing her heart out because her little baby will be fated to wander the earth. Who needed it?"

"You mean, you didn't sing to us, tuck us in, kiss us nighty night?" I ask, only half in jest.

"I had three hands," says mother sarcastically, "so I could do everything. Anyway, in those songs, first you tell the baby his misfortune, then you tell him to go to sleep. That's why Jewish children are so serious."

She begins to hum.

"Here's one, just to make sure the baby becomes a revolutionary in the cradle:

"*Schlof mayn kind*
schlof kesyder
zingen vill ich
dir a lid."

My mother smiles and reaches out to me. She has her arm around my shoulder:
"Sleep my child
Sleep safely
While I sing you a song.
"It's safe so far," smiles my mother. "Soon you'll see how it makes for a Red baby:

"*Die tayrste palatsn*
Die shenste hayzer
dos alts macht der orimen

The beautiful palaces
The gorgeous houses,
who makes them?
The workingman.
Who lives in them?
Only the rich."

"How does the song end?" I ask.

"The poor man lies in the cellar
where it's cold and damp
and he gets sick all over
but the rich
in his palace
lives in health."

*

"That's how it goes?" I ask.

"More or less," says Mama. "It's not an exact recipe."

"But, Mama," I argue, "the rich get sick too. There are well-to-do people in here with you."

"Don't be foolish, girl," says my mother. "How many poor people live until my age? Getting old is also a privilege of those who can afford it."

She lies back. Her hands begin to jerk. Her frown reappears.

"What about love songs, Ma?" I ask.

I am relentless. I want her to stay.

"What's your need?" says Mama. "You suddenly met somebody else? Anyway," she says, "from a Russian Jew, a love song is also a bitter song. The lovers separate, one to marry rich and live in a mansion with crystal chandeliers while the other is left behind, poor and cold, shivering like a leaf in winter."

She stops talking and dozes. She shivers like the leaf in winter. Her hand jerks. The other hand reaches to calm it.

"Sh, sh, *Mamale*," I croon.

I lullaby her until her frown disappears and the pair of hands nestle in each other.

"No invasive measures," my brother is checking with me again by phone. "Right?"

A long hesitation.

"Right," I say.

"That's what we agreed," my brother reminds me.

"Yes," I say softly.

"I've given the Nursing Home the telephone number of the mortuary," says my brother.

I do not comment. He is more efficient than I. And also more caring.

"I'm not the villain in this," he says. "We don't want her to be agitated. Right? And not in pain?"

Does that mean we loosen our grip? We don't wrestle so fiercely with the Angel?

Does that mean we speak of her in the past tense to get used to the sound of it?

Does that mean, if water fills the lungs, we don't increase the dosage of heart medicine?

If her sugar is high, we stop injections?

This long-distance call is filled with more silence than conversation.

"I read to her tonight," says my brother. "I don't know if she heard, but I read the whole *Jewish News* to her, column by column."

If one is sinking under the water, can one still hear the boat's motor?

"She seemed a little restless," says my brother, "so I sang to her."

"You did?" I'm startled. "What song?"

"A Yiddish song," my brother says.

"But you don't know Yiddish," I say.

"I took lessons," says my brother.

"How come?"

"What you're not given, you take," he says.

"How did it go?" I ask.

"The song?" he laughs.

Unlike me, he can carry a tune. I can carry a load. I can carry my own weight, but not a melody.

I had never heard his singing voice. Even over the phone I'm moved.

"Do you understand the meaning?" I ask.

"Oh, it's a folk tale about an old fisherman who went to sea, and he dreamt of fish and love. He ends up getting neither fish nor love."

My mother was right about Yiddish lullabies.

"Come fly by, sometime," I say.

"That could be," he tells me.

Somebody has to sing to me.

GHOST STORIES

I.

My Mother in the Mirror

SUPERIMPOSED UPON MY FACE IN THE MIRROR is my mother's. I am about to comb my hair, but here she is, brushing hers, her thick, wavy, white hair.

We quarrelled about hair.

"Don't wear your hair so short and flat, Mom," I said. "It's too mannish."

"Don't wear yours so wild and woolly," she would reply. "It's too girlish."

In the mirror, our arms go up and down in unison.

"Monkey See/Monkey Do," says Mom.

She pulls the hair forward from under her ears and forms spit curls.

"The return of the Nineteen Thirties," I say.

Actually, her hair looked very nice the last time I saw her.

"What dress is that?" I asked my brother. "I don't recognize it."

"He didn't like the one I brought," said my brother, "and said he had an extra."

"An extra?" I ask.

"Somebody must have brought two to choose from," says my brother.

"Gives her color," I say.

There she is, eyes closed, her glasses resting on her nose.

The glasses will rest there forever.

She's in somebody else's dress, with her hair brushed away from her forehead, high and fluffy.

"It's becoming that way, Mom," I say. "Keep that style."

Now, in the mirror, she brushes, parts her hair on the side, her two hands making a wave.

"I liked it better the other time," I tell her crankily.

I find hair in my comb.

"My hair's falling out," I tell my mother.

"My hair was always strong," she says. "Like my teeth."

"Do you like this length?" I ask her. "I just went to Barney's to have it cut."

"Barney's!" she says. "How can you afford Barney's?"

I flinch. I can never, ever, now or hereafter, tell my mother how much it costs at Barney's.

"I go to the barber in the neighborhood," she says.

We are in her bedroom. I'm cleaning out closet and dresser.

"Where's my face moisturizer?" she asks.

"I took it, Mother," I say.

"What else did you take?"

"The costume jewelry," I say.

"**You** gave it to me for Mother's Day," she says, "and—so fast—it's gone."

"I took hankies and scarves also," I tell her, looking in the pile I made for myself.

She sees a black plastic garbage bag.

"You threw out my stockings!" she exclaims. "Perfectly good, no-run stockings. And my panties, my bras."

"No one wants used underwear," I tell her.

"Plenty of people, believe me, would have appreciated stockings without runs, underwear laundered and folded," she says.

Could she be right? And about the girdle? Do people wear girdles?

She looks through the mirror at the dresser-top.

"You didn't take my Rose Petal cologne," she says.

"I don't like the scent," I say.

"You're the only one in the land that criticizes roses."

"I like something more subtle."

Suddenly, she reaches out, lifts the cologne, presses the nozzle and sprays me.

"Don't! Don't!" I raise my arms.

"Now," says Mother, "you smell just like me."

My mother is putting on her lipstick, a bright-red. She colors the top lip and presses her lips together. Then she takes a dab from her lips for her cheeks.

I take out my tube and outline my lips.

"I don't like that shade on you," says mother. "You look like a ghost."

"Mother," I say, "how's this?"

I wrap her pretty scarf around my neck. I fasten her earrings on my lobes. I push her bracelet onto my hand. I take a new pair of her stockings, still in the package, and roll them up my legs.

"Try my powder," she says.

"I don't wear powder," I tell her.

"I can't see you too clear," says my mother. "I've left my glasses."

"I'm going now, Mother," I say and lift my package of her belongings.

"Wait," she says. "It's getting cold. Take that warm coat."

"Whose coat is that?" I ask, about the old-fashioned dark wool with red fur collar, hanging in the garment bag.

"Your aunty's," says mother. "I hate things to go to waste. When she left, I went right over to the house and took her coat out of the closet. 'I'll wear it for you, my sister,' I said. Give a look in the pockets."

I put my hands into the pockets. Black leather gloves.

"Stay warm," says my mother.

The mirror is clear.

11.
Mother Visit

I used to speak long distance, coast-to-coast, to my mother at her retirement village and, later, nursing home. Now we sit side- by-side every Friday night and Saturday morning.

I brush the crimson velvet cushion next to me, to clear it of coats, prayer books, announcements.

"Do you have enough room, Mama?" I ask.

"Plenty," she says.

Sometimes she comments briefly on the service.

"Wonderful singing. On the other hand, the sermon's too long."

People will try to sit in my pew.

"This seat is taken," I always say.

She used to speak at greater length. She's grown terser, less patient.

As we begin preparing for the Mourner's Prayer, she's already pushing me out of my seat.

"Don't be the last to rise!" she says. "It makes a bad impression."

Sometimes I have to repeat a question.

"What will I do with the kid?" I ask. "The kid's in bad shape. Tell me, Mother."

"You can't ask me any more," she says. "You have to handle it by yourself."

"That's mean!" I say.

"That's where I am," says Mother.

In the autumn, I was expecting her favorite nephew, Daniel, good to her, bad to me.

"Daniel's coming for a visit," I say.

"Tell him hello for me," says mother.

"I'll kill him," I inform her.

"Don't kill Daniel!" she pleads.

After the visit with Daniel, Mother and I meet at our regular time and place.

"I didn't kill Daniel," I tell her. "I was nice to him."

"That's my good girl," she says.

She's happiest when it's a crowded Sabbath: a *Rosh Hodesh*, a new moon, plus a baby naming, plus the calling of a bridal couple to the altar, ending with a Bar or Bat Mitzvah.

"Today I got my money's worth," says Mama.

Soon it will be winter. She and I will come to the close of our mourning. I will have to relinquish her space to other congregants.

But, if I am her good girl and refrain from killing cousin Daniel, will I hear whispered blessings ruffling my hair, my life?

III.

Earth Tremors

"There's no stability to them," their grandmother said. "Just one, show me the one who's stable."

My job is to defend my offspring.

"The girl is very stable," I say. "She makes friends, loves her brother, designs clothes."

Their grandmother is thinking and frowning.

I continue. "The boy, he just loves children. He teaches in a playground, is kind to women and is lovable."

"Too lovable," their grandmother says. "A girl on each arm."

Apology is a part of motherhood. You apologize for a recent birthday present that went unacknowledged. If you go all the way back, you apologize to other mothers at the sandbox for the hitting with the shovel, the taking of the metal pail with the picture of a duck wearing a polka dot dress. You apologize for inattentiveness in grade school, being held back in Physical Education.

"Tell me something else good about them," says their grandmother.

"They like each other," I say. "They like the world."

"It's just not good enough," she says. "Someone has to make a living. Someone has to start a life. Someone has to choose which girl is on his arm."

We had never worried about stability.

At the table they tried to make one another laugh with outrageous puns and the drama of their daily lives.

I acknowledge their secret vices: in-group jokes, encapsulating themselves against the world of would-be friends, having the best vocabulary so everyone else would sound monosyllabic.

Another vice: scaring. The house prepared for Halloween with strange flashing creatures, projecting out onto the lawn, with a sound track they recorded themselves of hideous cackles and chains dragging. Little beggars were scared away.

Exploding fireworks, rockets, a rain of color from chemicals, all dangerous. The neighborhood children wanted to pour into the yard for the display but their parents tried to hold them back from such explosive children.

Despite their costumes at Halloween, I knew them behind their masks.

And, in the taped recording of Death's Castle, I knew each voice distinct. I have always recognized them: their baby voices, their adolescent changing ones. I know them sobbing, moaning and clanging at holiday time.

"They can't go on this way," their grandmother said.

But they did seem to be able to go on.

"The youngest isn't so young anymore," says the grandmother. "The oldest is even older. They don't go backwards and they don't go forwards."

"They're fine, just fine," I say.

"Go visit them," says the grandmother, "and put your foot down. Tell them, 'Things cannot go on this way.' Tell them, 'There must be stability.'"

I write down her words and visit them.

But they pun, joke, enlarge their vocabulary from a daily word calendar. They use words like *maleficent*, *malediction*, *vituperation*, *indefeasible*, *plaudit*, *imputation*. I cannot use their grandmother's old words on them.

Abruptly, in the midst of giving me advice, she dies, not knowing the end of things.

"It's not their fault," I say over her coffin. "I won't apologize."

It is evening. My children are in their rent-controlled apartments, eating produce from the wholesale market. Despite a roof over the head and vegetables on the table and becoming cultured, standing up at book stalls, they are in danger.

The earth has split under them.

I cannot reach them. Power lines are down. In the morning my phone rings. It's my family.

"Is every one safe?"

"We," they sing, "are on a holiday."

"Where? Where?"

"We're safe, Mom. Cool out," says the son.

"I was worried," I tell them.

"*We* were worried!" say her children.

They describe a surrealistic landscape, a city without lights, a walk without people. Neighbors of moon and stars.

"It's faulty here," says her punster son.

"Unstable," his sister continues the joke.

"We hunted each other out," says the boy, "all over the area."

"And there we were, right where we were supposed to be," says his sister.

I pause.

"Just you guys?" I ask.

"No loves," says her son. "I need my arms free to balance myself."

"Anybody have a job?" I ask.

"Mother!" they say.

They have jobs. The kind you have today in the city: half-time, part-time, adjunct-time, night-time.

"We didn't want you to worry," they chorus.

Behind them she hears the wail of fire engines. On the line she feels a trembling.

"What's that rumbling?" she asks.

"My stomach," says the joker.

"It's OK now," the sister says, "and the after-shocks aren't very big at all. We're going to stay together for a while. Nobody's going out to work."

Nobody's going to work?

"You'll need some money," I say.

"We'll pay you as soon as we get paid," says the girl.

"In the blink of an eye," says her son, "the snap of fingers."

"The cluck of the tongue," adds her merry daughter.

I hang up and, in a manner of speaking, dial their grandmother.

"Is this stable or is this stable?" I ask her.

COUSINS

MY MOTHER USED TO TELL US STORIES OF her village in Russia.

"The village was walled around and we lived within the walls," she said. "That was a time when we had fewer people to choose from. An uncle took a niece. An aunt chose her nephew, a cousin betrothed a cousin. And so, Dad and I fell in love."

Mom and Dad in love excited our curiosity.

"How could you tell that it was love?" we asked.

"By kissing," Mother said.

"I felt her soft lips under mine," said Dad, "and how was I to know she would be mine forever?"

My parents lived happily ever after, dying a year-and-a-half apart. My father went first and the memory of that kiss lingered and sent my mother after him.

One day in the synagogue this past winter, I have bad news for her.

"Mother," I say, as I slip into the row of our pew,

"Cousin Benny died."

"Not old," she said, "Not near old. How did it happen?"

I'm not able to tell her.

"Over-work," I say.

"Such a worthwhile person," says Mother. Her shoulders sag. She coughs slightly. "A nice fellow, besides being a relative."

I don't say that he had developed an aneurism in the lungs, had choked on his own blood or that the apartment was speckled with that arching blood. It hit the walls, venetian blinds, even the papers on his desk.

"He didn't live well," says Mother. "A doctor and he lived like a student."

Like an aging student, in a studio apartment, unpainted for decades, the varnish on the floor long gone. His bookcases were jammed with videotapes and books. The videotapes were copied from the Metropolitan Opera television broadcasts. The books were second-hand paperback. On top shelves were his hardcover medical school books and one large art book with color reproductions, a present from the staff at his hospital.

As for burying him, try to find a suit not threadbare.

"Why did he live like that?" Mother wonders.

The services are about to begin. The congregant sings a *nigun*, a wordless song, to get us settled. The rabbi's eyes are looking around accusingly at those among us who are still chattering.

*

Benny is practicing the violin. I reluctantly practice the piano. Benny practices with the intent to master. I practice, distracted by metronome and clock.

When the required half-hour is over, I rush to his flat in the neighborhood and call to him from the sidewalk.

He sticks his head out.

"I'm practicing," he says. "Don't interrupt."

"Cousins," I say, "are supposed to interrupt."

I teach Benny to dance.

"Move in place, Benny."

"How can I move and be in place?"

"Your hips, move your hips."

"Show me."

I say, "I place my hands here on your hips. Lift hips, move, shift the pelvis."

We dance the Samba.

"Move, Benny, slowly, slowly."

"Like this?" asks Ben.

His eyes are hazel, his hair straight, soft brown.

"Not so stiff. All of you. Move."

"I can feel you, cousin," says Benny. "All of you."

I teach Benny to kiss. I have only just learned. We bump noses, miss the mouth and keep angling our heads so we can approach one another.

When our lips do meet, it is the way my parents described their first kiss. I didn't know boys had such soft lips. I didn't know a string of spittle would still connect us after we broke off the kiss.

*

"So what's going to happen to his property?" my mother asks.

She was always practical. Life came first. Death, when it approached, was attended to. If someone were left over, my mother went to work match-making.

"I don't know if Cousin Benny has property," I say.

"He worked all his life and he was a doctor. How could he not have property?" asks my mother.

She looks sideways at me.

"Maybe you'll get it. He was always partial to you. More than to your brothers."

"Yours is the only mail on your cousin's otherwise blank desk," the Detective had said.

The Detective had phoned from the precinct near the Projects.

"Yours is the one photo in the apartment. You are, as far as I can tell, his only living relative."

"I am not his only living relative," I say. "I have brothers."

The Detective said, "There's no evidence of anyone else where he's concerned. You might try to find out the name of his attorney. Until then, we will regard you as the executor of his estate."

Benny, born in low rental neighborhoods, at his death living in the projects, with an "estate"?

I'm too shocked to laugh.

His interest in being a doctor was life-long.

We play Doctor in my basement.

"Where are Aunty and Uncle and the boys?"

"Out," I say.

"OK, this dark basement is the hospital."

"Who's sick?" I ask.

"You are."

"What's the matter with me?"

"First I have to examine you."

"You're tickling me," I object. "Now I'll tickle you."

"You can't," says Benny. "I'm the doctor and you're the nurse. The nurse can never tickle the doctor."

"Why?"

"It's against the rules," says Benny. "I have to perform this medical experiment. Unbutton your blouse."

He begins to lick my tips of nipples.

"Gross!" I hit him. "My whole chest is wet."

"One day, cousin," says Benny, "you'll ask me to do that."

"One day, cousin," I promise Benny, "you'll be dead because you will try to touch my blouse and I will kill you."

"Tell me what Benny died of," says Mom, the following week. "I've been shocked all week and forgot to ask."

"There's confusion," I say.

"That's Benny," says Mom.

"They thought it was a heart attack at first. In fact, on his death certificate, it says heart attack."

"Then it's a heart attack," my mother declares.

"How could a medical document be wrong?"

"It couldn't be Benny," I tell the Detective on the phone. "Benny was a health freak."

"The body was found on the premises," says the Detective. "I want you to identify the body."

"Did he wear glasses?"

"Not at the time of death."

"Did he have grey eyes?"

"Who could tell, Miss?"

"Did he have a dimple in his chin?"

"I can't recall," says the Detective.

"You have the wrong party," I say and hang up.

The Detective calls back.

"He lives in your cousin's building. He lives in your cousin's apartment. He appears to be your cousin's age. The likelihood is—"

"That he isn't my cousin. An intruder, a robber, maybe a roommate."

The Detective sighs. "Will you view the photos?"

The glossies are of someone with closed eyes, no glasses, no discernible dimple in the chin, the face covered with dark smears.

"Wrong party," I say.

Eventually I identify him.

"Benny would never allow himself to have a heart attack," says Mom. "Didn't he eat nuts and grass?"

"Grains," I say.

"And he was all the time running up and down the stairs when there was a perfectly good elevator in his building. What floor did he live on? Fifteenth? I never went to visit him there. Up and down, down and up. Tennis. Swimming. Are you sure it was Benny?"

"Then the Detective said—"

"Detective?" Mother's voice goes up.

There is a sudden silence in the synagogue. Prayers have been disrupted.

I whisper. "From the local precinct. He was called in when the neighbors complained."

"The neighbors complained about Benny?"

I can't continue. I pause.

"Go on. Go on," she insists.

"It took a while to discover him," I say.

Mother is crying. I didn't know you could cry after you go. I knew your hair and nails grew. But I didn't know tears still poured.

"Alone?" she asks. "He died alone. The poor boy."

We sit side by side, holding hands.

"But then he was a loner," she says. "Why didn't he ever marry? Do you know?"

She looks at me sharply.

I shake my head.

"His poor parents," she says. "They had a genius on their hands and they were such simple people. They didn't know what to do with him."

"So they sent him away," I say.

"They're sending me away," Benny says, "at thirteen!"

"What did you do wrong?"

"I know secrets," says Benny.

"About the family? Did you tell the secrets?" I ask.

"No," he says, "but they're afraid I will."

"Who are *they*?"

"My mother, my father."

"Because we played Doctor."

"They don't know that," says Benny. "Because I'm smart, they're shipping me out."

"They don't want you to be smart?" I ask.

"They do want me to be smart, stupid," Benny tells me. "That's why I have to go."

"I don't get it."

"Thirteen years old and I'm being sent away."

"Where? Reform school? Military school?"

"The university," says Benny, "and I have to live in the dormitories."

I try to comfort him. I stroke his hand. I coo at him.

"Stop that!" says Benny and I snatch my hand away. "You sound like a pigeon. Don't pet me. You'll give me pigeon lice."

We end up fighting, as we always do.

"I'm happy you're being sent away."

Benny says, "I feel like I've done something bad, so bad they can't just spank me or ground me."

And he cries.

So I stroke him again and say, "Benny, I wish it was me going. You hear that? I wish I was you, away from this neighborhood, away from this family, to the university."

I have tears in my eyes too.

Benny is mean as always.

"You can't go," he tells me. "You don't know the nominative case. You don't know the subjunctive. You'll never be admitted to the university."

"Go and don't bother writing," I say.

Then he sits on the porch glider, his head hanging down, and I sit next to him. I always forgive him.

"My parents are mad because I'm different," he says.

I've known him so long he doesn't seem different, just Benny.

"They're throwing me out because I'm not short and don't speak with an accent."

I tell him, "Then my parents would throw me out too."

"My father doesn't want me looking down on him. That's where it all started. I was nine, looking down at his bald spot. No, it started before. I was behind the crib bars and talking to him."

I never knew when Benny was making it up.

"So, there I was in the crib and I said, 'Poppa, hello! Let me out of this cage.'"

"'He talks already. Is that normal?' asked my father. 'Shh, don't tell,' said my Mama.

"'Mama,' I told her, 'I'm slow walking but fast talking so help me over the top of the crib and we can talk together.'

"'He's a freak,' says my Papa. 'Don't take him out or the neighbors will think something from the devil got into our house.'

"'Don't be silly, parents,' I said reasonably. 'I'm just

speaking a little early. Don't keep me in to punish me.'"

I interrupt Benny.

"What's so secret about that? I knew you were an early talker. They were proud of it. Mother told me they always boasted about it while I was still saying one word at a time."

"Wrong as usual," says Benny. "Your mother had you out rain or shine, up and down the block, at the parks, the playgrounds. I was kept in my crib, in my playpen, behind bars."

"That's the whole secret?"

"There's more, worse," said Benny. "They didn't read to me. I read to them."

"That means"—I'm shocked—"that Aunty and Uncle can't read. How does your father work?"

"A tailor needs to know numbers, not words."

"What do they do if they don't read?"

"They listen to the radio, stupid," says Benny. "They think we're *One Man's Family*. They think I'm Baby Snooks. They think we're *The Goldbergs*. So, because I don't fit into the radio console, they're sending me to the university."

Benny is sobbing on the glider and I keep pushing the glider back and forth until he wipes his eyes and goes home.

"So what's happening with Benny?" Mother asks. "It's a few weeks already. How was the funeral? Where? Who came? How big was the crowd?"

"I didn't know his friends, Mom," I say. "Samuel

and I buried him in New Jersey where the plot wasn't expensive. We had to take money out of our savings account for the burial."

"Not responsible, like Dad and I were," says Mom. "Plot, perpetual care, everything.'

"You're a *mensch*," I tell her. "Totally."

Mother is pleased. She's not used to compliments from me.

"That's the main thing," she says, "to be a *mensch*."

She will not be distracted, however, from the subject of the conversation. "So, tell the funeral."

"They came, his friends. Animal people, veggy people, bimbo people, people people."

"What are animal people?" asks my mother.

"Animal rights people in cloth shoes."

"He had a tender heart," says my mother. "Especially for animals. It came from doing horrible things to them in that lab. He didn't want to do it but they made him. So what are people people?"

"The health care group. His colleagues, the doctors, nurses, social workers."

"So he had some decent friends. I'm glad to hear it. And bimbo people?"

"All boobs and no brains."

"Cousin Benny?" Mother exclaims. "Who would have thought?"

We listen to the familiar synagogue music. Sometimes a new melody is brought in which the congregation resists. They enjoy their service like Enna Jetticks shoes, lace-up comfortable, unchanging.

"So," Mother turns to me, "who gets his estate? The animals, the vegetables, the doctors and nurses or the bimbos? But why not you? Why in the world not you?"

I shake my head. What has Cousin Benny ever given me in my life?

"What did you say at the grave?" Mom asks. "You did go to the cemetery, didn't you?"

It was a dreadfully rainy day, the ground muddy, our shoes sinking in, covered with mud.

"We talked about his going to the university at thirteen and that ruined his life. He was always fighting being the prodigy forever after."

"He never fit anywhere," Mom agrees. "Too young or too old. Too young to be a college student, too old to be a hippy. His poor life! What did you bury him in?"

"One of his suits," I say.

I don't mention the frayed cuffs.

"I bet it was from his Bar Mitzvah," says Mother. "He never cared how he looked. And see where it got him. Buried like a pauper. So what's happening on that front?"

"The Detective said we're the executors."

"Maybe he put aside a nest egg," says Mom. "He couldn't have worked all those years for nothing. Wouldn't that be nice, my girl, if he thought of you?"

We spoke constantly about being cousins.

"My parents and your parents were first cousins," Benny said. "Who knows what that did to us genetically?"

I said, "It made you nuts. It gave you those golden hands."

Then Benny asked, "Is it still illegal for cousins to marry?"

"Yes," I say. "The marriage of my mother and father is illegal."

Benny asks, "But if cousins love one another?"

"They are allowed to kiss," I say, "on the cheek, on both cheeks, lightly on the lips."

Benny wants to know if we could break the rules.

"No," I tell him.

"What are the rules?" he asks.

"Cousins are allowed to share the past and the present," I tell him.

"What about the future?" Ben wants to know.

"And to disturb one another's future."

He laughs. "Is that the rule?"

"The unbroken rule," I say.

"Till death do us part?"

"Yes, till death do us part."

But we had years of the past and the present. Before Cousin Benny exploded.

"What do you think of my baby, Ben?"

The baby is perfect, gurgling, dimpling.

"Babies are not my area of specialization," he tells me.

"It's not a specialty. It's a cousin," I say.

"Second cousin to be accurate," says Ben. "Second-hand cousin. I never thought of you as a mother.

You're suddenly older than I am."

"I'm a year younger," I remind him.

"If you were my age, you'd have time for me," says Ben.

"I have no time for anything," I tell him.

"That's you all over," he says and leaves without eating. I remove his place setting from the table.

"You deserve his consideration," my mother is saying.

"Why do I deserve it?" I ask.

"You were with him all that time when the other children couldn't stand him. He was a smart aleck, a show-off. But you lugged him with you everywhere— even later, when he was in college, you took him to parties. You taught him to dance. Did he ever have a girlfriend, a date? I remember now, he said one girl broke his heart. A mystery girl."

"Yes," I say.

Another time Ben phones and I invite him to dinner, as always forgetting how he had acted before.

"Can't I just see you? How *are* you?"

"In the family way again," I tell him.

"I know that way," says Benny in his nasty voice, "the ballooning stomach, arched back, straddled walk."

"It's a good thing you never became an OB/GYN then," I say.

Benny tells me, "I never went for babies, mewling, spewing, spitting up."

"Then it's a good thing you didn't become a father."

"A very good thing," says Benny, "a good thing I became a doctor and all because of you."

"Because of me?"

"The basement," says Benny. "Remember?"

I am unusually quiet at Saturday's long, three-hour service.

Mother asks, "Is there anything you're not telling me, something I should know?"

"Benny hated his mother and father," I tell her. "He didn't have a single photo of them in his apartment. Or of anyone."

But me. Dancing at some party long ago.

"The poor parents," says my mother. "They did their best. They talked of nothing but him. They thought of nothing but him. And he left them and never phoned, never wrote. Not a birthday, an anniversary. Forget Mother's and Father's Day. But, when the father died, not even to go to the funeral. That's more than angry. They didn't deserve to be treated that way."

"And you?" I ask. "How was he to you?"

"Nice, very nice," says Mom. "He could have used some of that nice for his parents. You know what he did? I told him I was interested in health. He went right out and got me a life-time subscription to *Prevention Magazine*. I kept it in the bathroom and read it. It was my bible." She laughs a little. "Now the life-time subscription is over."

We sit quietly.

Mother looks up suddenly. "What happened to his violin? How he loved music! Remember how he would leave the violin at our house and play late at night after coming back from the hospital?"

"Come to a concert," Benny phones. "I have a solo with the Doctors' Orchestra."
"What will I do with the baby?"
"Leave the baby," he says simply.
So I leave the baby and go to the concert.
"Come to the After-Glow," he pleads as the last applause dies away. "Everyone will be there."
"I won't be there," I tell him.
Samuel is sitting.
"It's all right," said Samuel. "It's for family."
"But you're all I have of family," says Benny.
I go to the After-Glow so he'll have family.
"Want to dance?" he asks.
"I've forgotten how," I tell him.
He puts his arm around me.
"I haven't. Move. Move your hips."
"Like this?"
"Just like that," he says. "A little closer."
Suddenly he hurls me away from him.
"Your blouse!" he says, "You're soaking wet. You're soaking me."
We don't meet again for a long time.

And now I'm his Executor.
We had gone to his sealed apartment. The Detective lifted the duck tape from the doorway.

"You'll not be able to bear it more than a few min-utes," he said. We both wore masks.

The blood-soaked mattress had finally been removed, but the floor was still sticky. I grabbed quickly what looked important: his files, a notebook, his address book.

All week I phone the names in his worn address book to inform the people that Ben died. Then I wait as they weep or are incredulous, comfort them, and tell the story all over again.

Ben keeps dying. I dream of Ben, that he is dying and coughing and I try to prop him up. I dream we are in his bed in embrace. He coughs then vomits. I am covered with blood like a new-born. I try to look into Ben's eyes but they are stuck shut.

I come to services worn the next week. Mother launches right into the topic.

"He didn't have a private practice," says Mama. "He didn't have the heart for it. Couldn't get near any-one. But he did work all his life, didn't he? And doc-tors don't earn peanuts."

We were looking through his files for anything, the name of a lawyer, a lover, an executor. We were look-ing for peanuts.

And we found curious notations.

We found a bequest of monies to the very universi-ty that admitted him at thirteen, that he hated and always spoke against. And yet they received a grant of thousands of dollars. He gave to PETA, People for the Ethical Treatment of Animals. Checks every year. He contributed to Doctors for a Nuclear Freeze and to a Buddhist Temple.

I tell this to mother.

"He's squandering your money!" my mother exclaims.

Then we both laugh.

"He was a nice fellow," says Mom. "Let's do him justice. More than nice. Brilliant. It was frightening. Like sparks were coming out of his eyes, off the top of his head. I used to think he was a freak—you know, from another planet. He knew about every subject: medical, psychological, mathematical, musical. There was nothing he had not read. When he came to stay over, while he was a resident in the hospital near us, I felt like I was getting a whole semester's college from him. Besides, he was a boy with golden hands."

I climb up the tree in the corner vacant lot. Benny stands beneath it screaming up at me.

"Get down from there. You'll fall."

"No, I won't," I say. "You climb up!"

"I've got to take care of my hands," says Benny.

"Golden hands," I imitate his mother. "Little prodigy. Stay down there, sissy boy!"

"Stay up there 'til you die, tomboy!" says Benny.

Mother is looking at me when I stand for the Mourner's Prayer.

"You know," she says, "Cousin Benny doesn't have anybody to say the *kaddish* for him."

"I know," I tell her when I sit down.

"I'm willing to share," says Mother. "You can keep us both in mind at the same time."

"I don't think I can," I tell her.

"If I'm not selfish," she says, "why should you be?"

Physician friends call from his hospital to inform me of the results of the autopsy that was performed before his funeral.

"He died from an embolism in his lungs that traveled."

"A travelling embolism," I say, "Like a frequent flyer?"

"Ben," I say, after phoning repeatedly and never finding anyone there, "Where have you been?"

"Went to Louisiana for a medical meeting. Saw the Bayou," he says.

"As in 'How's by you?'"

"Went to Greece for a conference on pediatric psychiatry; went to Israel for the conference, 'Freud's Children;' went to Thailand to learn the latest in psychopharmacology; went to Guadalajara for a seminar on 'Autism after Bruno Bettleheim.'"

"You spent your money on those trips?"

"Of course not," says Ben. "Paid for."

"What did you do in Thailand?"

"Bought a suit. It got lost with my luggage."

"In Greece?"

"I did the sun."

"In Guadalajara?"

"Danced."

I said, "I taught you to dance."

"Yes," says Ben, "among other things."

"What other things?"

"You taught me to fit against you, to measure myself by you. When you left me, I left myself."

Mother asks, "What's new with the family?"

"The usual," I say.

I find she doesn't want details unless it's about a baby's eating habits or a new love who's come into the family. She does not need to hear family tales any more. They've all been told.

"Ben," I say, "you never ask me how I am, how the children are, how the marriage is."

He says, "We'll make a bargain. Tell me how you are and don't tell me how your marriage or children are."

"Oh," I say nastily, "you want to know how everyone else's children are feeling. Every stranger's offspring, every little *meshuganeh* finds his way into your office. Every brain-damaged, retarded, autistic kid is on your lap."

"You're just jealous," says Cousin Ben.

"I hear he did good work in his field," says Mother. "Give credit where credit is due. As a son, nothing. As a social person, forget it. But with children—maybe he felt an affinity with them."

*

Ben told me about Teddy. He took his violin to the psychiatric ward for Teddy to pluck the strings.

"'Now,' I tell Teddy, 'I'm putting the violin into its own case, in its bed.'"

Teddy cannot go to bed. He is often strapped down. Or he wanders all night.

Ben tells Teddy a story about a quiet boy in the forest, a boy who does not speak. Teddy sits near Ben, not trusting to be touched. Ben tells about the white-footed field mouse who came to the boy. And the boy did not move, did not speak. And a hummingbird fluttered near the boy. And a rabbit nibbled the grass around the boy. And who was the boy? Teddy!

Ben said, "I told him a deer came, with antlers, and nuzzled Teddy's hand. And slowly, slowly Teddy was nuzzling mine."

"For a man," says Mama, "who worked with children, he had no patience for them. It's good he didn't have them. Though, for a while, I thought the two of you would make a pair. But then it's unhealthy for cousins to marry." She laughs. "Except in my case."

I once said to Ben, "I want to ask you something."
"Ask," he said.
"Don't you love someone?"
"Actually, I do."
"Who?"
"My clients."
"A woman," I said. "Don't you love a woman?"

And Ben said, "Once I loved a girl. I'd have given anything to her. I'd have stopped growing for her."

"The Detective called," I tell Mama one Friday night. "He said I have to prepare for Kinship Day."

"I never heard of it." Mama giggles. "Is it like Valentine's Day? Sweetest Day?"

"I have to present papers, proof of relationship in court. My Tree of Life, the Detective said."

"Where are the papers?" asks my mother. "I had some in the bank box. I kept nothing at home after we moved to the retirement village. Benny's folks are gone. Your brothers know nothing about it. I can't remember, my dear girl. I sort of went off there at the end. Sorry. I can't remember to help you."

"I have to get a lawyer," I say.

"Another expense," says Mama. "Cousin Benny turned out to be a pest."

In another week, I tell Mama that the lawyer is searching through Ben's papers, most of them already removed from his apartment. The lawyer said Benny must have liked to play Hide-and- Seek.

"He did!" says Mama. "I remember now. 'Come in O, come in O, if you don't come in you're out!' Keeping you up long after bedtime and you'd come in flushed, just ready to catch a cold."

She is bristling with old annoyance.

I say, "I feel like Benny's out in the ozone, giving us clues one at a time. The lawyer found pay checks at his hospital, checks he hadn't picked up in months. Then he found that Cousin Ben had a hundred thousand in pension."

"Well, it pays to live frugally," says Mama, changing her tune.

"He couldn't care less about money," I remember.

"That's right," Mama agrees. "He used patients' checks as book marks. If he accidentally found the check in the book, by then it was too late to cash. I found a few in our own bookcase from the times he visited."

"Games," I say. "He's playing games."

We play Monopoly on our glider. I win.

"Your swing needs oiling and you're cheating," says Benny.

"You can't cheat in Monopoly," I tell him.

"If you're not cheating," Benny asks, "why do you always win?"

I tell him, "I play smarter than you."

"It can't be," says Ben. "Play something else."

We play Michigan Rummy and Benny doesn't trust me to shuffle so he shuffles the deck.

"Rummy!" I soon call.

"You cheated!" says Benny.

"You didn't shuffle good," I explain. "I got all matching suits."

And then I beat him at other board games. Dominoes was the easiest. So Ben shows me how to play Chess and I Check-Mate him.

When Ben remembers, years later, he remembers wrong.

Ben says, "I won all the games."

"What a liar !" I'm shocked. "*I* won all the board games we played."

"You don't remember," he insists.

"I've had time to remember," I say. "Only one thing I don't remember. How come I let you get smarter than me?"

"You were smart enough for a girl," Mama soothes me when I tell her about the summers of playing games. "At some time you should start losing and let them win, and, in the end, you win big."

"Like what?"

"Like a life's partner," she says.

"Mama!"

We seldom see one another, Ben and I, and when we do, he takes me to some veggy place with paper plates and we talk. Or I listen and he talks. Usually about Teddy.

"'Teddy,' he tells the story, 'I will sit here on this chair and wait as you bump, bump, bump your head against the wall. I have a present. Look, a helmet! Like a football player. Put on the helmet, Teddy, and the bumping will not hurt your head. You can bump through people, through walls, through all of your nightmares if you wear this helmet. That's it, my boy.'

"Oh," says Ben thankfully, "the child can bang his head and not hurt his brain. Thanks to Whomever, to Whatever!"

*

"What's doing with the lawyer?" Mama asks.

"He's going through investment slips, deposits, bank accounts. And the Detective, for some reason, is still after me.

"'We think it was an aneurism,' he says. 'But we can't be sure.'"

"What's an aneurism?" Mama asks.

"They told me it was a pathological, blood-filled dilation of a blood vessel."

"I knew there was something pathological about Benny," says Mom. "Reading all that Freud. Living a secret life."

"I know all your secret places," Benny whispers to me in the basement.

"How do you know?"

"I'm the doctor."

I tell him, "All doctors do is take out your tonsils."

"Doctor cousins are different. They're explorers as well."

"Will we always be cousins, Benny?"

"Till death do us part," says Benny.

His first year at the university, Benny calls me.

"I've got a choice job in the lab."

"Do you wear a white lab coat like a scientist?"

"I wear a white coat like a mad scientist."

We laugh and, from then on, I call him Doctor Frankenstein.

95

He phones more often, each call sadder than the one before.

"I get blood all over my white coat, like a butcher," he says.

"Aw, c'mon."

"I kill," says Benny. "That's what they do in the lab."

"What do you kill?" I ask.

"I kill mice; I kill rabbits, and there are worse things I do to cats."

I think he's kidding.

"Cats," I laugh. "My father's favorite joke is, 'Who sleeps with cats? Mrs. Katz.'"

"You'll hate me when I tell you," says Benny.

And he tells me that he gives kitties dishes of food with alcohol in the dish until pretty soon the cat won't eat. It just wants to drink.

"My professor is experimenting. He wants to make the little furries into boozers. He wants to make the four paws alkies. And he asks me to write down, every day, carefully, how they walk, if they stumble, if they stop eating, if they are in a stupor."

"He's nuts, Ben," I say. "Get away from him."

"He's nuts and I'm complicitous."

"What's complicitous, Ben?"

"Get away from me. You don't know anything. Not words. Not what I'm doing. Nothing."

"I didn't call you. You called me."

"Stay out of my life," he says as usual.

"That's easy, kitty-killer," I tell him.

*

We speak when I'm to get married. He's in medical school.

"Who is he?" he asks.

I tell him.

"I don't know him," says Ben. "And I don't go to the weddings of people I don't know."

I don't finish college.

"How's the weather?" my mother asks. "I lost track."

"Record-breaking warmth this autumn," I tell her. "And then record-breaking cold. Both unseasonable."

"Not where we retired in California," says Mama. "Every day seasonable."

He still phoned periodically to give me major information.

"I'm a vegan," says Ben. "No meat or poultry. No leather shoes. No more torture of animals."

"The whole word is full of torture," I tell him. "In every country somebody is crying out for help and you worry about animals."

I have become a scold in our relationship.

"Where's tenderness, mother of earth?" he asks.

"Forget it," I tell him.

He never forgets unless he wants to.

"What about primates?" he says. "Opposing thumbs, remember? Like us. How about keeping primates from being given immune-deficiency diseases? Or cats and rabbits from being tortured?"

"I'm trying to keep the kids from getting measles," I tell him, "and whooping cough and chicken pox. Don't phone me about primates."

"Creep," says Ben.

The years pass. We meet in various places in town.

I see him at a good restaurant.

"Hi, Ben," I say. "I thought you just ate on paper plates."

Ben says, "Meet the girlfriend. Philipa, this is my cousin. We were raised together, like brother and sister."

I meet him at a train station.

"Ben! What are you doing at the station?"

Ben says, "Meet my girlfriend, Yoko. Yoko, this is my first cousin."

Once we met at an airport lounge.

"Ben," I ask, "Embarking or debarking?"

"Meet my companion. Loretta, say hello to my little cousin."

And at a branch library.

"Ben!" I say. "What are you doing here?"

"Looking something up," he says. "Meet Sachiko. Sachiko, meet my favorite cousin."

Or, another year, at a Woody Allen movie, in the days when I went to them.

"Cousin!" says Ben. "Meet Clarissa. Clarissa, say hello. We're kissing kin."

I tell a little of this to my mother.

"Did he choose them for rhyming names?" asks Mama. "Clarissa, Loretta, Sachiko, Yoko."

"The thing is," I tell her, "the lawyer says his handling of the case is eating up my profits."

Ben was by himself walking down the street.
"Alone?" I asked, my eyebrows lifted.
"You made me change my life," he said.
"From what to what?"
I fell into his trap again.
"From here to there," Ben said. "When you moved, I had to move."
"Liar!" I said. "You liar. You lived forever in that dump."

The lawyer tells me he has found something interesting in Ben's lists of: Books to Read, Operas to Hear, Women to Date. There is also another listing, that of his stocks.
"You could be sitting on easy street," the lawyer says, "when we get it all together."
"Mama," I say, "Ben wouldn't have thought to put me on easy street. He never sent a present, not birthday, wedding, baby gift. Not a nickel could he bear to spend on me."
"It's never too late to change," says Mama.
"Guess what, Mama? It's too late."
"But where is his will?" the lawyer keeps asking.
"He'll make the will out to a Yoko or Clarissa, or to the soft shoe group, and every kitty and puppy will have an extra meal," I tell the lawyer.

*

The phone rings.

"I can't sleep," says Ben.

"I was," I whisper. "Why did you awaken me?"

"If I can't sleep," he says, "why should you?"

I creep out of bed to the other room, then return to the bedroom to hang up the phone.

"What time is it?" I finally whisper.

"By the lit-up hands of my clock, 3:00 am," he tells me.

I've forgotten the time in my life.

"I'll be feeding the baby next."

"There are no babies left."

"You're right! They left me long ago."

"You have no one to feed," says Ben.

"I left my bed and my partner to answer the phone."

"I was your original partner," says Ben. "And I'll be your partner until you die."

I hear a call from the bedroom.

"Is something wrong?" Samuel asks.

"Goodby, Ben," I say. "Don't call me at night any more. And not too often during the day."

I had forgotten another late phone call, years before.

"My father died," Benny said.

"Uncle died? The first of our parents to go."

"I talked to my mother."

"That's the least you could do."

"I invited her to visit."

"You didn't go back to bury your father?"

"My dear, ignorant cousin, I had buried him long ago."

"Speaking of unforgiving!" I say.

"Who didn't I forgive?" asks Ben.

"You and your whole life," I tell him.

He invites me up to his dump. I hesitate, then take the subway uptown.

Of course, he has no food in the apartment.

"What did you invite me up for?" I ask him, careful where I seat myself.

The blinds have not been dusted in a decade. The floor should not be walked on barefoot.

"I want to show you photos of my trips," he says.

The photos are from ThailandGudalajaraIsrael-HongKong.

"I can see *The National Geographic* for photos," I say.

"I wanted to tell you what I learned about the world."

"I can go to a lecture."

"I wanted to tell you," says Ben, "that no matter how far I traveled, or who I met, I thought of you."

"Don't tell me that," I say.

"I just want to talk to you."

"Ben," I say, "I can hear talk from the neighboring pillow on my own bed. The pillow does not travel. It lies there steadily, next to me, whispering at night the news of the day."

"I'm not the daily press," says Ben. "You see me when you see me."

And he opens his arms. Across that dirty floor, on those dirty sheets, we love, and add yet more stains to the bed linens. Then I rise, grab my purse and rush out the door.

"I'm never coming back here!" I say. "Never!"

"Oh yes you will," says Ben.

"Mama," I tell her, "the lawyer located the will. It was stuck in one of his books, along with old pay checks from the hospital."

Mama begins to pat my head excitedly. I have no expression.

"I see," she says and her hand drops.

"So, tell me. I'm curious. Who then? The Bimbo People? The Animal People? The Veggie People? The People People?"

"None of the above except for some small checks I told you about."

"Well?"

"You want to know who gets the boot, the loot, the bundle and boodle?" I say. "Orphans."

We are silent. Even the singing doesn't move us. When the congregation rises, I tiredly pull myself up.

"It figures," says Mama.

"High IQ Orphans," I tell her, "a special organization he founded."

"That's how Benny thought of himself," says Mama. "What happened with Kinship Day and Family Tree?"

"I couldn't locate anything, Ma."

"I could have thrown it out when I moved," says Mama. "It was a big move to California from the Midwest and I wasn't always careful with the papers."

She's sad. Then hopeful.

"Are you going to fight the will?"

"Have I a chance without a family tree and against

orphans?"

"That's it? That's really all there is?"

"A little more to report. The Homeless have his socks and underwear. The Literacy Campaign has his second-hand paperbacks. Senior Citizens gets his TV, VCR and video tapes. The disabled get his exercise bike. Science has his body. And the prodigy orphans get his portfolio."

"Nothing for you?" asks Mama. "All those meals I fed him. All those hours spent listening to him."

"I get his apartment," I say.

"In the Projects?" asks Mama.

"A tiny, unpainted, falling-apart apartment."

"Why, for God's sake?" Then she reconsiders. "So sell it and be done with it."

"His will stipulates that I can't sell the place."

"What does he want from you?" Mother asks. "He always wanted something."

"I expect that he wants me to unlock the door, go inside that empty apartment and think of him."

"Some nerve. That's the craziest thing I ever heard of," says Mama. "Will you do that?"

"No. I won't think of him any more. That was too much in my life."

"You'll let the place stay vacant?"

"Maybe I'll go there and say, in every corner, 'Ben, I'm not going to think about you. You're cleared out of my life.' And then I'll leave and lock the door behind me."

"Be practical. Rent it to some student. Maybe a

medical student at one of the hospitals uptown."

We have nothing really to say. Our main topic is exhausted.

"And the *Kaddish*?"

"He's on his own, Mom."

"He was never on his own," says Mama. "He didn't know how to be a *mensch*. I'm not possessive. Fridays you can say it for Benny and Saturday morning for me."

She tugs. I rise tiredly to recite the words of praise repeated four times during the service and yet necessary for remembrance.

In my parents' village they could trust only the family. Outsiders could betray. The uncle watched his niece become a woman. The cousins watched each other very closely and every day. But it is not allowed. It is never allowed. Even when death parts them.

Mother sits down heavily.

"It was my fault," she said. "You came from cousins. I should have watched you very closely and every day. You'll stand next to me and think of him and I'll be there, at your side, to protect you."

MY MOTHER, THE MOVIE STAR.

MY MOTHER AND I SIT SIDE BY SIDE, SHE on a velvety cushion. It is my last chance to elicit information about her young married years, her taste, her favorite colors.

"What were your colors, Mama?" I ask.

"Dubonnet and aquamarine," she says promptly.

"But you never wore them. You always bought them for me," I say.

"One of us had to wear them," she says.

We have to maintain a certain decorum in the synagogue, but, during the sermon or the singing of psalms, we whisper.

"Your favorite film?"

"Movie, you mean movie. I liked them all."

"That's no help," I say.

"The Women," she remembers. "Best of all, I loved *The Women.*"

"I heard bad things about it."

"Don't listen to bad things," says my mother. "It had

all the top stars—Joan Crawford, Rosalind Russell, Paulette Goddard, and, starring, Norma Shearer."

The worshippers in the pews ahead and behind us are becoming irritated.

"Don't talk during services," says a regular, who always rests his coat on my bench.

Mama and I stare straight ahead.

"I'll tell you something you don't know," says mother after a while. "They told me I looked like Norma Shearer."

There is mother next to me, shrunken, her face lined, looking like *her* mother at eighty-six.

"That's what they called me, Norma Shearer," says my mother. "Remember the picture in the living room, drawn by the boardwalk artist in Atlantic City?"

It was there throughout my childhood, long after the garment she posed in had faded.

"I was wearing my embroidered top, with red, yellow, blue flowers on a black background over the black silk skirt."

"The skirt doesn't show," I say, in the cranky interest of accuracy.

"My hair was pinned back behind my ears. Exactly Norma Shearer."

The first thing I did, when her place was cleared, was to lift that portrait off the nail and carry it home with me. Her face is soft and young. She is slender, her hair wavy. I owed it to my mother to see *The Women*.

In the week between services, I rented *The Women*. I hated it.

"Why, Mama?" I ask. "Why that film?"

"Movie," says my mother.

"It's sexist, classist——."

"Pish posh," says my mother. "The main thing is, Norma won. She was a wonderful mother, a wonderful wife and, by the end, she beat out that floozy, Joan Crawford."

We are both silent.

"I had hair like Norma Shearer," says mother. "Mine was dark and curly too. And my eyes"—she has the grace to hesitate—"were hazel like hers. I never had her figure but I never had the time to have a figure."

She is smoothing the velvet of her seat.

"That was over fifty years ago," she says. "What difference does it make now?"

"Shh!" says the portly man whose portly coat cushions my back.

"*Ein andere velt.*" My mother is dreamily in the past.

"What was that other world?" I ask.

I want to do know everything.

"We all looked like somebody else then," says my mother dreamily.

Her faces smoothes out like the wrinkles from the velvet cushion.

"There was our crowd, your father's crowd actually, and the leader of that group was Rex, short for Rexford. Rex looked like William Powell. Remember him? *The Thin Man* with Myrna Loy? *My Man Godfrey* with Carol Lombard? Rex was a dapper, slender fellow, with a thin mustache, very sophisticated, William Powell to the T."

"Who else was in the group?" I ask. "What other movie stars?"

"I don't know if you even will recognize their names," says mother. "My friend, Ray, a schoolteacher, was skinny. They called her Zazu Pitts. And Mimi, the wife of a math teacher, was very pert, like Janet Gaynor of *A Star is Born* with Mr. Frederick March. In our crowd, there was the insurance salesman's wife, Ruby. They called her Joan Crawford because she was proud, broad-shouldered and tall."

She smiles. "I was more the old-fashioned type. After all, I came from the Old World."

"Did any of them come from anywhere else?" I ask.

"They were all Americans. That wasn't the only thing that separated us."

She is twisting her thin wedding band. It used to cut into her hand when she was heavy-bodied. Now she turns it easily on her finger.

"They were educated. I didn't finish high school."

"Was it hard for you with them?"

"Of course," says my mother. "How would you like to be the foreigner in your group?"

A week goes by. My mother and I wait until the end of services when it is time for me to rise and honor her. That's her favorite part. She rests her hand upon mine when it's coming near that part.

"What did William Powell do for you?" I ask her during the meditation and final prayer.

"In the movies or in life?" she asks. "In the movies he thrilled me, Mr. Sophistication. In life, Rex was Dad's favorite in all the world. They were everywhere together. If one began a book, there was the other, writing Chapter Two. If one had an idea, the other promoted it. They were a funny pair, like Mutt and Jeff from the comics—tall thin Rex and your short father."

"Rex was at your house a lot?"

"Not *a lot*. All the time is more like it."

"Did you mind?"

"Your Dad loved him. How could I mind?"

My mother is dowdy. She always was. Maybe her hair was curly, her grey eyes storm clouds, but her clothes were Second Basement, Month-End sale.

"I was different from the other women in the group," says my mother. "They had hats and gloves. Some had jobs. Very responsible. Teachers. Book-keepers. But I had something they didn't. I was the only one who could welcome all of them."

She is proud of this.

"If Rex suggested to them, 'Let's meet at your place or your place,' they'd say, 'Oh, it's not convenient,' or 'The place is a mess,' or 'I'd have to rush to get the food prepared and you know I hate to rush.' No sooner had Rex asked me, 'Will you?' then, one, two three, I'd make a tuna salad with hard-boiled eggs and sweet pickles. I'd mix together a batch of poppy-seed cookies, put up coffee, set the bridge table, and we'd all sit around for hours and talk."

"Still talking," says the man behind me, who waits until the last minute to lift his coat off the back of my seat.

"You too, Mama?" I can't keep quiet. "You sat around and talked?"

"I'd sit around and listen."

"And what were the women like? Were they nice to you?"

"Sometimes." Mother turns her face away. "Yes, Ray, the teacher, was wonderful to me. She always said, 'Sit down, Bronya. Take a load off your feet.'"

"And the others?"

"The men were polite, educated, you know, like your father. And the women were a little bit snobbish."

"Did they insult you?"

"Oh no!" says my mother.

The congregation files out.

"*Au revoir*," says Mama to me.

During the week I think of my mother serving the crowd, wearing an apron over a house dress. They would sit at mother's table, all those decades ago, eating her cookies, holding out their cups for a refill and ignoring her.

I was not Mama's kind of housekeeper, always at the ready. She chose domestic gifts for my birthday, a blender, Dust Buster, sewing machine. Not on purpose, but I never seemed to get the knack for busting the dust, blending ingredients or French seaming. Do I still disappoint her?

Even so, maybe I have another chance after all these years. The next Friday, I sit next to my mother, feeling my hand held, the pages of my prayer book fluttering to the right section.

"Tell me more about Rex," I say.

She smiles. "He played our piano by ear. He made up the music. He made up languages. He made us laugh."

"You, too, Mama? You laughed.?"

"Why not?" says my mother.

Mother smiled. She did not laugh in company. At her kitchen table, telling family stories, she would laugh uproariously. But she would not seem to get the joke when she was out in public.

The women of her husband's group would look at her critically. She did not share their lives. She was never in the beauty parlor. She could not shop with them, for she was a bargain hunter. And she was a drag when the group wanted to eat out since she kept kosher.

"It was Ruby," says my mother, "who told me I looked like Norma Shearer."

Ruby smoked cigarettes in a long holder.

Why did Ruby tell my mother that? Because Ruby never had the group at her elegant apartment? Or did she look upon my mother's light eyes, wavy hair, sweet smile and feel, for a moment, kindly?

I begin to think of Norma Shearer as my mother. I rent another Norma Shearer film the next week, a film that came out also in 1939, *Idiot's Delight*. The MGM lion roars once again. In *Idiot's Delight*, Norma Shearer, like my mother, had a Russian accent.

"I took up drama in Russia," says my mother, when I tell her I saw Norma Shearer as a Russian countess.

"I was no slouch either. You don't know about your mother. You think I was always a homebody. When I was a young girl living in Russia, in a small town, I had occasion to go to a private school for a couple of years. There I learned dancing, French, acting. I loved acting! My greatest wish was to be an actress. Then I came here, worked in the laundry and forgot about acting. Still," she says, "who knows? Maybe I could have been Norma Shearer if I'd had Perc Westmore to make me up and Adrian to clothe me back then in 1939."

"What were you doing back then in the Thirties?" I asked her.

"Give us a break," says the widow in the row ahead.

But remembering is my mother's job.

"What was I doing in the Thirties? I'll tell you. Living like a dog," says my mother. "Living in the back of my in-laws' store in Paradise Valley, the Negro section of Detroit. And, suddenly, your brother gets sick. A double mastoid. I woke up and could hear him breathing very heavily. In the morning I called a pediatrician. I told him that I had a very sick child, that he was running a high fever and that I did not have the money right now but I swore that at the very first job my husband got, I would send him a check. The doctor bawled me out, saying, how dare I ask him to come without money?"

"The bastard!"

"Did you ever?" asks the widow, turning to look at me.

"And then we called our friend Rex," my mother says in my ear. "He knew the doctor. Rex phoned us and said the doctor was coming right over. The doctor lanced both ears and told us that he'd be over again to see the baby the following day. The first part-time job my husband got, I sent the check."

"Were you happy, Mother?"

"What kind of a question is that?" Mother snaps. "And why now, of all times?"

She looks down at her hands, so thin they seem to melt into her skirt. "Of all times!"

She pauses. "Yes and no," she says. "We were young. That's happiness. But we were poor. That's unhappiness. Poverty isn't a musical, you know, with little Miss Shirley Temple tap dancing."

"I hated Shirley Temple," I say meanly.

"You were jealous, simply jealous," says mother. "You couldn't dimple, you couldn't memorize. All those mornings I made sausage curls.

"There was Esther Williams in the water, Sonia Henie on the ice and both in films. There was such opportunity! Shirley was waning, Jane Withers was becoming a has-been, and you wouldn't practice."

Suddenly mother says, "Step Shuffle Hop Down Down."

"You remembered the steps!" I say.

"Who practiced tap dancing in the basement with you? Two wooden legs you had even then."

"I disappointed you, Mother?"

It is clear to me she is weighing the dripping comb,

the money spent on lessons and tap shoes against the rest of my life.

"You've improved," she says.

"Do me a favor," says the woman in front of us, "Take out a membership in another synagogue."

"Some people!" says my mother. "I always got along with my neighbors before this. Rich, poor, good, bad, you get along."

"But you didn't get along during the Depression."

"Nothing is all bad," says mother. "The baby boy got well. You grew into a smart big sister. We moved into my mother's house and her place was suddenly like a palace, though your father and I slept in the hall, your grandmother in the kitchen, and boarders took up the bedrooms. It was a rough time but everyone got along and there were no arguments or quarrels."

I wonder if there were indeed such a time, a family squeezed together, with boarders, and no money and no quarrelling.

"Your father and Rex sang a funny song," says mother.

She sings into my ear:
"I sing in praise of college,
of M.A.'s and Ph.D's,
But in pursuit of knowledge,
we are starving by degrees."

"What did you do for fun?" I ask her.

"That's all you can think about?" says my mother. "Fun?"

She remembers half-a-century ago.

"The movies," she says, "a double bill, changing twice a week, regular as clock work, previews, cartoons, newsreels included. Sometimes also dishes. The gangster films—James Cagney and Paul Muni, Spencer Tracy and Edward G. Robinson. Romance. Humor, *Modern Times*, with Charlie Chaplin and Paulette Goddard, Chaplin's mistress both on and off screen. Everything you ever dreamed about was up there on the screen."

"Why do you bother coming to services?" asks the widow in the row ahead.

"My sentiments exactly," says the man in the row behind.

We become silent, but Saturday morning services are long: prayers of praise and petition and thanks and repentence. We're standing up, sitting down, standing again, sitting, up and down like a yoyo, so, in no time at all, standing up or sitting down, mother and I are at it again.

"Did you go out a lot with Rex?" I ask.

I remember him romantically though I was a child when he left. "Rex would come to our house practically every day. We would sit until midnight or later discussing current affairs. Often he would bring friends. Two or three times a week he would take us to parties, meetings, lectures, movies or museums or to his apartment."

"Rex had money while Dad was out of work?"

"Rex had money until he lost his job, as they all did,

for a number of reasons. One was a teacher and the principal sat in on his social science class and had him fired as a Red and he never taught again. One was too poor to finish medical school and he did menial labor until there was no more menial labor for hire. One was so burdened with his family and parents and grandparents that he went into a police station and asked to be institutionalized. There was no one you could envy. It wasn't fun, my girl."

"Then the Depression ended, and everything was all right?" I ask.

"The Depression ended," says my mother, "but everything wasn't all right. Rex had moved to California, which figures for a Mr. William Powell. There was a job for him out there in merchandizing. He hated it, poor man. The last thing he did, before he left, was to make a movie of you tap dancing to *Shuffle Off to Buffalo*. You were grinning with your front teeth missing."

I'm disappointed in this description. I wanted Max to feel nostalgic about me too.

"I dressed you and put a big bow in your hair. You tap danced, arms swinging, the bow bouncing up and down. The sun was gleaming on those shiny tap shoes. You were a star of the home movie screen," says my mother.

It's clear this was less than she had hoped from me.

"Why didn't you and Dad go?" I ask.

"Your father was frightened. The Depression made cowards of us all," says mother.

She is crying. Her eyes have sunken deeply into her head, the tears staying there on the fleshy ledge.

"Your father would look out of the window for twenty-five years, saying, 'There's no one like Rex.' And in Los Angeles, Rex would say, every day, 'There's only one like him.' Rex blamed his wife for making him move away from his crowd, his closest friend."

"And what of you?" I ask. "Did Dad blame you?"

"No, but he said, over and over, 'We were David and Jonathan.'"

"And then?"

"And then came World War Two and then Korea and then Rex died. And then your Dad died. And that ended that. They never found anyone like the other."

"But you were there for Dad!"

"I couldn't sing funny songs in made-up languages. I couldn't pretend to play the piano. I wasn't an educated person. We seldom saw the old crowd again."

"You should have followed Rex, then," I tell her.

"You're telling me what I should have done?" cries my mother. "You can't do what you haven't the strength to do. What were we, the Oakies, like in the movie, *Grapes of Wrath*, moving to California? What were we going to do there? Pick fruit, like Henry Fonda and Jane Darwin?"

"I myself ask you a favor," says the man in the row behind, lumping his coat more over my seat. "Don't wish me a good Sabbath."

"All the way across the country, I couldn't go," says

my mother. "I couldn't leave my mother and brothers, while they lived. I didn't feel I could uproot you kids."

"You could have," I say. "We would have liked California." Mama's grown so thin, she's almost invisible on her velvet pillow.

"Besides," says my mother, "out there, they would have known for sure that I wasn't Norma Shearer."

FAT AND FED UP

NEXT TO ME IN THE PEW IS MY MOTHER. She once occupied two seats, two velvet cushions. Now, one seat is roomy.

Mama touches her face.

"Lend me your mirror," she says.

She peers into it.

"Losing all that weight wrinkled my face. Also, hairs are growing out of my chin."

"You look all right, Mama," I say.

After all, she *is* an old woman.

"Bring your skin moisturizer next time," Mama orders. "It's so dry in here it's like sitting on a radiator."

She is impatient during the announcements from the pulpit: an AIDS luncheon, visit to the local hospital, a study group, a concert.

"It's nice they bother having services," Mama says.

These days her memory is sharp and her tongue sharper.

She was an unselfconscious, loving woman in the old days.

Or could I have been wrong?

I remember going downtown shopping with her as a child, falling asleep against her large, soft breasts on that long bus ride home, and she never stirring beneath my heavy head.

I remember coming from school, not asking how her day went but plunging into my own. The afternoon sun shown on her face as she lifted it smiling, to listen to me.

I remember her stroking my head, holding my hand, until even a few months ago.

I have seen her most recently in summer climate. Before that, when we both lived in the Midwest, we met by accident one cold winter day in the check-out line of a supermarket. I stood behind her wondering who this person was, with a pin head under a small kerchief, and an old coat that strained at the buttons.

"Look at you, Mother!" I said.

"I'm only shopping," said my mother. "I'm not going to the opera."

Behind us stood mother's neighbor.

"Missus, is that you?" asked the neighbor. "I never would have known."

"Pish posh," said my mother, turning to face the cashier.

She left winter, that tight kerchief, her old coat and the neighbor, for a retirement village in southern California.

Nobody was over-weight in her retirement village. The swimming pool guard checked the residents for high blood pressure before he let them soak in the jacuzzi. The athletic coach weighed the sports participants before he allowed them to exercise.

Weight was the danger in the village for there was no theft or assault. From its inception, the village was fenced, gated and patrolled.

I was visiting her retirement home and we walked together, she huffing and puffing over a slight incline.

"You'll get yourself in trouble carrying all that weight," called a passing motorist.

Church and synagogue goers carried their Pritikin diet along with their prayer book.

Unlike the villagers who *spatziered* at night in linen suits, my mother sat on her patio, wearing her house dress, not moving.

I am ashamed of her. It occurs to me that I have always been.

Of her girth and girdle, her flesh everywhere, climbing out of her bra, folding into a tire over her girdle. Her flesh was so active it needed restraints.

Of her accent. Her second language, English, was grammatical, but her pronunciation Old World. She would substitute "w" for "v"; "The whale on the hat." She used pronouns indiscriminately.

Of her unstylish appearance. Clothes were selected from the sales rack, regardless of fit. In California she wore only mumus or house dresses.

As a conformist child, I was ashamed of every way in which she was comfortable with herself.

*

We sit quietly now, intending to get to know one another in the months left.

She turns suddenly. "I was always ashamed of you," Mama tells me.

"Of *me*? Why?" I am astounded.

"Your silly laugh, for one thing," says Mama. "Then your flighty ways. Even your hair, hairy all over, hairy legs, arm pits, eyebrows."

"Why didn't you say anything?" I asked her. "I would have changed."

"You would have changed your hyena laugh?"

"Sure."

"Your flighty ways."

"I'd try."

"Your hair."

"No, not my hair."

Not my unruly, wild hair.

"Also your housekeeping," says my mother.

I sit thinking this over. She had given me a blender and sewing machine over the years but I learned neither to stitch nor to blend.

"You didn't like me?" I ask her.

"Not very much," she says.

"I didn't know," I tell her.

"Well, that's good," she says. "Then no harm done."

We rise in praise of the Almighty.

"Funny," says my mother, "to think He constantly needs praising. It's never enough for Him."

In the service the cantor begins a lively melody to the command about observing the Sabbath. My mother beats her hand in time against the pew before her. She had always loved singing. I remember her in the Women's Choir, her mouth opened, eyes concentrated on the male conductor. Even in a large auditorium with all the singers in dark robes, we had no trouble identifying her. She took up two spaces in the middle.

We don't talk during the Meditation but I am filled with questions.

"Why didn't you like me?" I ask for the third time.

"You were snotty with me," says Mother. "Nice to your father but scornful with me. The truth is, you thought you were better than I."

Her grammar is impeccable.

"I did," I admit.

"Why?" asks my mother, still hurt. "I read everything. I talked the news over with your father. I kept a nice house. With what could you possibly find fault?"

"You were largely uninformed," I tell her. "You made a big deal of little things."

I am surprised to find myself with a long list of complaints.

"The meal was your main subject of conversation. And you didn't listen to what anybody said."

"Like you, for instance," snaps my mother.

"You ate with your mouth open," I say.

"So we didn't like each other," says my mother.

Then all this is hypocritical, these Friday-night, Saturday-morning meetings, this year of mourning.

"I'm sorry I hurt your feelings, Ma," I say. "I wasn't aware."

"That's just it," says my mother. "I was invisible to you."

We are sitting down. My book is opened. She knows the service by heart.

The page number is announced. I turn to it.

"Look!" says my mother, "It says today, the New Moon!"

The new moon proclaimed in song, and repeated three times.

"To pray for a new month always used to cheer me up," says my mother. "If it didn't work out, soon enough, twenty-eight days later, on this calendar, another month came along. It was as regular as a period."

She looks at me curiously.

"Speaking of which, got the pause that refreshes yet?" she asks.

"It's beginning," I tell her.

"It's a snap." She snaps her fingers. "Don't give it a second thought."

"I feel as if I were plugged into an electrical outlet," I tell her.

"The flushing and flashing," she says, "that's it. 'Open the window,' I'd order your father. 'Close the window.' 'Open,' 'close,' all night long. 'Blankets. Cover me.' Then I threw off the blankets."

"Did you have an emotional time of it?" I shyly ask her. "The empty nest syndrome."

We never had spoken intimately.

"Not a bit," says my mother. "Couldn't wait for you birds to fly away. I always liked your father's company best and I got him finally to myself."

One of her favorite songs is being sung. Instead of singing, she mouths the words.

"Have you lost your voice?" I ask gently.

"I've sung those songs thousands of times," she says yawning. "By now they bore me."

From my reading of her files, this surprises me.

Mama continues.

"If He's our Father, our Shield, how come he didn't remember a little thing like shielding us during the Holocaust."

"Now you're asking?" I say.

"Better late than never," says mother.

We rise for the final blessing. Mother wiggles her fingers distractedly at me.

"Ta ta."

All week I think of mother as the questioner of God. That was not what I was discovering in the papers she left me.

This week I also sleep and dream of eating meals with her. I dream of all the food piled on the table at the same time, the main course, chicken or roast, the soup, the salad. Nobody rose to bring on the next course. The food lay in front of us to be consumed without pause.

She judged herself by the accomplishments and shortcomings of others. She was ashamed of her lack of education but had overweening pride in her keen eyesight and good hearing.

"I can read a sign a mile away," she said, pointing to my Dad who wore thick glasses and held the newspaper up against his nose.

"I can hear a pin drop," she boasted, in contrast to my Dad's increasing difficulty in hearing. In their retirement village, he bought hearing aids for both ears and a special connection for the telephone.

Unlike her neighbors in the Midwest, she enjoyed the neighbors in the retirement village.

"Turn the tv down," she always ordered my Dad, who had the set turned up full volume for his news and sports. "What will the neighbors say?"

"Who are your neighbors?" I asked her once when I visited.

"On one side is a lovely man whose wife is dying of cancer. On the other side, that lively lady is having a boyfriend over for the weekend. 'Don't judge me,' she said to me, 'It's the twentieth century!'"

"At least," I say.

My father smiles. He loves this eighty-year-old lady who skips down the path past their attached house, drives beyond the speed limit, and carries her camera on its shoulder strap around the world.

"That's life here," said Mama. "You find your last lover or take your last breath."

Soon, Dad's hearing aids were pulled out of his ears, his glasses put away in their case. On the bier, despite cosmetics, he had deep indentations from the nose-rests.

A year and a half later, she also took her last breath.

My brother put their house up for sale. I made trips to the village to help clear the closets.

"Look at this," said my brother, "every dress she ever owned. Every suit he ever wore."

My father's shirts and suits were all of a size. His weight was constant from the time of his marriage until, sixty-one years later, his death.

I found dresses of my mother's of every size hanging protected by cellophane, from a 9 to a 44. I found each pair of shoes she bought, 7 ½ to 10. There were dresses she had taken in and dresses she had to let out.

"Nothing is thrown away," said my brother. "Here is every letter you ever wrote her, and, in this envelope, all the birthday and Mother's Day cards the children and I sent her."

I left her house for the last time with a 9 × 12 envelope addressed to me.

I look inside at the loose sheets of paper. I glance and return them to the envelope.

The next week my mother asks, "What have you been reading lately? I always like to hear about books. Biography is my favorite."

"I'm reading a biography," I tell her, "of Virginia Woolf."

"Forget those English anti-Semites," says my mother. "I left you a bookcase full of books including a biography of David Ben Gurian, an autobiography by Golda, another by Abba, and a third by Sharansky."

Actually, I've been reading them but I don't want to give her the pleasure.

"By the way," my mother asks, "did you read any of the papers I left in the envelope for you?"

"Not all," I tell her.

"The longer you wait, the yellower the paper," she says. "Like me."

"I'll read the papers," I promise quickly.

"And you'll see," says Mama, "how you wronged me."

At the end of the service as everyone is shaking hands and wishing one another a good Sabbath, I turn away from my mother. Why did she have to leave me with a mean mouth?

Finally, I open the manilla envelope. It is filled with sheets of typing paper, scraps of paper, cut out articles. I select one sheet, addressed to a group called, "OA's":

> "It was their fault. They are to blame. I was only 120 pounds through my early marriage and even with my children. I was not [she crosses out 'stocky' and writes] obese. But, as the children grew to teen-agers, they invited many friends home. I started spending a lot of time in cooking and baking and then eating the left-overs. I became a human garbage disposal."

"Wrong, Ma," I say to myself. "Wrong on every count. We did not have many friends. My brother was shy. He went straight home from school and locked his door. I had a few strays. All a fiction for your OA's."

"Mama," I say the following Friday, "I didn't make you fat."

"First I was pregnant with you," she says. "Then I drank beer so I'd have rich milk for you. Then I'd eat so I could keep up my strength for you. Ditto, for your brother. Then you both grew up and demanded

132

sweets, cookies, cakes. Then you had friends with the same demands."

"Mother," I say, "some people are just heavy and some are skinny. I didn't exactly appreciate being called Skinny Minnie in high school."

"People can be made fat," says my mother. "Everything is there in the world to fatten you up. Take, for instance, television where people are employed solely to eat unhealthy food in front of your eyes."

I have a memory, maybe even from the past year, of going to visit my mother in her loneliness. First thing she asked was, "Are you hungry?" She prepared her usual lunch, the one she made for herself and Dad for years, a tuna sandwich and borscht with sour cream, cheese blintzes and poppy seed cookies. And then mother sat down at the table and ate again to keep me company.

This Friday, my mother says, "There were those I could pour out my heart to, not to you. You didn't care for me. You didn't care what a struggle I was in."

"I didn't realize," I said.

"A smart girl, but a dumb girl," says mother.

"You talked to Dad?"

"You can't talk to a scrawny person."

"You talked to overweights?"

"Overweights Anonymous," says mother.

"The OA's," I say.

"Your Dad would tease, 'You gals going to chew the fat?' I would ignore him, but every week, the same joke. A teaser doesn't let up."

I had read, during the past week, her "confession" to the OA's:

> Because I had the horrible experience of my early years of famine in Russia, I constantly, in my later years, kept buying and storing foods for fear there might be a scarcity. When I had my family, and had to prepare for four, I used to prepare, instead, for eight or ten.

She hoarded. Our attic held boxes of toilet paper and canned goods that were on sale at the supermarket. We would climb the attic stairs to bring down the fruit cocktail, Bumble Bee Salmon or tuna, green beans, canned corn, canned pineapple. We ate For Sale.

"What did you do with the OA's?" I ask.

"I was Book Chairman," Mama says, "reviewing books on our subject. You could get a psychological view, a deprived childhood view, a nutritional view like from an overly starchy childhood. You could get a spiritual view, like an autobiography on how this woman found self-esteem by looking Above rather than remembering how she had been a little barrel for years. Wherever you looked people were suffering and bloated."

A short man on the altar is struggling to lift the uneven Torah. There's more weight on one roller than the other. The man lifts the scroll, tilts and almost drops it. Others rush to right the both of them.

My mother finds this amusing.

"Why did they ask a small man?" she says. "They could have gotten a big woman."

She goes back to her duties for the OA's.

"I reviewed *Diary of a Food Addict*, *Fat and Fed Up* and *How to Be Your Own Best Friend*."

During the week I discovered, besides my mother's remarks to her group, that she was also a seeker of God in prayers not found in our *siddur*, prayer book.

"I learned how to chair a meeting," says mother. "You know how shy I was and public speaking didn't come naturally, especially with my accent. But, I'd take in a deep breath and begin, 'Good morning. Welcome to the Monday Morning OA meeting. To open the meeting will you give your names?'

"I would identify myself and go around the room. Then we would stand in a circle and say the serenity prayer. You know it," she says to me. "'God grant me the serenity/to accept the things I cannot change,' and so on.

"It was a big job to be Book Chairman. I was responsible for getting them in the mood to talk. For instance I would say:

> "'We will repeat our mantra, *Abstinence*. Think that your life will change, your tummy will be flat and you'll feel like you're walking on air.'"

I recognize that introduction from the notes in her collected papers.

"Why didn't you go to Weight Watchers, Mama? Wouldn't that have been easier."

"No," said Mama. "At Weight Watchers they weighed you. They made shame shame if you gained. They whistled and applauded if you lost. I wanted a quiet group of fellow sufferers."

I think about my mother as a sufferer and myself as no comforter.

When the service ends, Mama busses me. All around us people are shaking hands with strangers, kissing family and friends.

"Take good care of yourself," says my mother. "You're looking peaked. You don't want to end up like me."

And she laughs.

This week I read more prayers among the papers my mother clipped. "Ten Commandments for Wives," from *Dear Abby*'s advice column in the daily press profoundly shocked me.

> "The Ten Commandments for Wives"
> 1. Defile not thy body neither with excessive foods, tobacco or alcohol that thy days may be long in the house which thy husband provideth for thee.
> 2. Put thy husband before thy mother, thy father, thy daughter and thy son, for he is thy lifelong companion.
> 3. Thou shalt not nag.
> 4. Permit no one to tell thee thou art having a hard time of it...

"Poor Mama," I said to myself.

From *Psychology Today* is advice on, "How to Control Yourself":

> "Control yourself, control your temper, your emotions, your weight."

When I arrive for services, my mother is eagerly awaiting me. She's turned toward the door, waves and grins when she sees me. Her teeth have turned dark

from neglect these last years, but her smile is so eager I
leave my coat on, hurrying to her.

"I missed you," she says.

"Mother," I say, "if you weren't working so hard to
control yourself, you wouldn't have had to eat."

"What is this?" asks my mother. "Women's Lib?
The chief cause of divorce in the world."

I don't like her again.

"I hurt your feelings," says Mama, softer. "I forgot
you were one of them."

"Who can talk to you?" I say, flushed with anger.

In a minute, we have turned from love to long-
standing disagreement.

"Let's just not talk," I say, "not sitting and not
standing."

"Suit yourself," says my mother.

The cantor is singing:

"I will lift up my eyes unto the hills
from whence cometh my help."

"Pretty tune," says Mother. "I don't know it."

It's a musical medley tonight.

The cantor sings:

"The entire world
is a narrow bridge
But the important thing
is not to be afraid."

"He sounds like the OA's," says Mama.

We grin at each other.

"Ask me for a recipe," she says suddenly.

"You gave me some before," I remind her. "Stuffed cabbage and meat borscht and tuna salad."

"Did I tell you how to make Mandel Brot, Matzo Brei, Carrot Tsimmes?'"

"If I asked," I tell her, "you would dismiss me with, 'Drop in a pinch of this and a pinch of that.'"

My mother pinches me and shrieks with laughter.

"Didn't you want me to learn how to cook?" I ask her.

"Maybe not," says mama. "Maybe I was protecting you."

"I know your recipes," I say. "I've found your holiday cookbook."

"Could you really read them?" she asks. "I was remembering them for you, writing them in this notebook in blue ink, and then, clumsy me with my fat fingers, I knocked over a glass of water on the notebook, and the ink spread over the pages. Goodby, recipes."

"I made them out," I say.

"If you're so smart," says my mother, "how do you make Mandel Brot?"

"Ingredients," I list, "are eggs, sugar, salad oil, vanilla, flour, baking powder, salt, walnuts."

I pause to remember.

"Not bad so far," says mother. "What else?"

"Raisins, maraschino cherries, cinnamon and sugar."

Mother beams. "Well-recited. You always had a good memory. Now Passover's coming, tell me," she pauses, and springs it, "Matzo Brei."

"I'd ask and you'd say, 'Take matzo and fry it and you've got matzo brie.'"

"It's true," says my mother. "But what else did you learn?"

"Matzo, eggs, skimmed milk, salt, pepper."

"You could also cut in onions," says mother.

"It wasn't in the recipe."

"So add it to the recipe."

"Okay," I say.

"A plus," says mother.

There's a buzz of activity on the altar. An elderly man is saying the prayer for someone sick.

"Poor fellow," says mother, "his wife, no doubt."

She listens closely to the Hebrew. She shakes her head. "A topsy-turvy world, a grandfather praying for his grandbaby."

The congregation buzzes with sympathy.

"All right," says mother, "Carrot Tsimmas."

She squints her eyes. She thinks she'll trick me.

"Three kinds," I say. "First, carrots, squash and cinnamon. Second, carrots, raisins, apples. Finally, carrots, pineapple and maraschino cherries."

"A perfect score!" crows my mother.

She squints at me again, then quickly, "Salmon Loaf, Matzo Kugel, Passover Cake."

I recite for her.

She folds her hands and closes her eyes.

"I got it," she says. "An inspiration. A real inspiration from the Almighty. You're always trying for the best seller on the side or a movie script."

"I'm doing all right," I say defensively. "I've managed to live."

"Feed, but not feast," she says. "How about a non-fiction best seller?"

She does a little hop when we're instructed to rise for a prayer.

"A special kind of cookbook," she says, sitting down again. "*My* recipes, typed from my handwritten notebook and also new material I'll tell you these coming months, combined with the final ingredient, my memoir."

"Lots of cookbooks are combined with memories," I say.

"I'm not finished," says my mother. "Your whole life you interrupted."

I'm silent.

So is she. "I'm thinking of a title," she says.

"*Feeding the Face*," I tell her.

"Don't be *pruste*," she berates.

I imagine that means rude, crude.

"*An Appetite for Life*," she says.

"Wasn't that an old film? I ask. "How about, *Fat and Fed Up*?"

"You've got a mean streak to you," says my mother. "I'm trying to help you out after I'm totally gone and you're resisting me."

I resist all week. She's awaiting my arrival eagerly.

"You found my memoir?" she asks. "All we have to do is stick in recipes."

"Like squeezed between the pogrom and the

typhus epidemic, the recipe for beet borscht? In Dad's words, we can title the book, *Chewing the Fat*."

"Skinny people have no joy in them." Her eyes are gleaming. "How about, *Munchies for Mortals? More than a Life-Time of Cooking? Heavenly Eating?*"

"*Heavenly Eating*!" We crack up.

"What would the OA's say to this celebration of eating?" I ask.

"They should *lieg in drerd*!"

In hell is where she wants to put her old OA's!

"And all that praying for self-control and obedience and submission?"

"Pish posh," says my mother. "This is the Twentieth Century."

"At least," I agree.

"So, is it a bargain?"

"Only in my spare time," I tell her.

"It's you and me together, kid," says mother. "What a team!"

We settle in for one of the various melodies with which to greet the bride of Sabbath, Slavic or Sephardic or Arabic in origin.

"But why do you think it will be so popular?" I ask.

"It's got a gimmick," says my mother, "the first posthumous cookbook."

She smiles through the rest of the service.

As the day darkens and the service comes to an end, she turns to me.

"I'm beginning to like you," she says.

SECRETS

THERE IS A SET TIME TO MOURN AND TO BE done with it.

According to Jewish custom, the mourner intercedes between the dead and heaven for eleven months. During the last month of the year of mourning the deceased pleads for herself.

That's the way it was and that is the way I thought it would be.

My mother and I sit cozily together on every Friday night and Saturday morning. She loves this highly ornamented synagogue with its heavy chandeliers and stained glass windows replete with the names of the donors.

"A palace," my mother said.

"You like it?" I ask her.

"Yes, considering the circumstances," says Mama.

Parishioners try to squeeze into her place each week but I insist, "This seat is already taken."

This isn't her regular house of worship. That was

in her Orange County retirement community where, when the need arose, a synagogue was hastily erected out of cinder blocks. Its major purpose was honoring the passing of its own membership.

Mama looks around. "Money talks," she says.

A man on our bench looks up from his book frowning.

"What does money say?" I whisper.

"It says, 'I'm well-to-do, cock-a-doodle-doo, and here's my name on the window with the sun shining through,'" says Mama.

I'm adjusting myself on the bench, folding my coat, removing the prayer book. I look at the page number of the book the man on my right is holding.

He, in turn, looks annoyed and covers the page.

"Don't talk to the Cossack," says my mother of our pewmate. She leans back. "So, what's new?" she asks me.

"Unseasonably warm," I inform her.

"That's how it was all year in southern California," says my mother. "My roses blossomed, opened wide, died. Not long after, there they were, raring to go again."

The man next to me snaps shut his prayer book and moves.

My mother giggles. "He'll be back. He forgot his coat."

She makes herself comfortable with the extra space. I discourage latecomers from sitting in our row.

"What's new in the family?"

"Nothing," I say.

She folds her hands.

"They've got all the time in the world," she says sarcastically. "They'll never get old."

"Stop it, Mama," I say. "Put in an extra word to the good for them."

"I could," says Mama proudly. "I have some pull up there, you know."

She fits the red velvet cushion more securely under her.

"Who? Dad?" I ask.

"*Pull*, not companionship," says Mama. "What do you think you're here for? To remind Him of pull, pulling me up, so to speak."

The former pewmate reappears and yanks his coat from our row.

"Go in health!" my mother calls after him.

His back twitches at us.

The sexton comes down the aisle.

"We've had a complaint about you," he informs me.

Mother and I are subdued.

"Work okay?" she asks, barely moving her lips.

"Okay," I say tersely.

"We should settle things," says Mom.

"What things?"

"Between us."

"That's dangerous," I say.

"I'll tell if you tell," she says.

The sexton looks in our direction. I am staring straight ahead.

"Nothing to tell," I say.

"When I was seventeen," says my mother, "I was in love."

I put down the prayer book.

"With whom? Where?"

"You sound like your Dad, may he rest in peace. His journalism motto was: Who? What? When? Where? Why? The five W's, he called them."

"All right," I say. "Tell all five."

"Where: Poland. When: After World War One. Who? A young gentleman. Why? Because I was a nice young lady."

"Before Dad?" I ask loyally.

"There *was* such a time." Mother closes her prayer book. "It's a whole *meiseh*, not just a who who."

"The lover," I remind her.

"Seventy years ago," says Mom, "like yesterday."

"Tell."

The Torah passes at this moment. Mother is pushing me to the end of the aisle to kiss it.

"I love this part best on Saturdays," says Mom. "The Torah marches by all dressed up in its velvet robe, and we crowd to kiss it for luck."

The Torah is returned to the Ark.

"The story," I remind her.

"Once upon a time," says mother, "there was a young girl, her mother, her big sister, spoiled as you shall see, who were in Poland for two years on the way out of Russia, awaiting their visas to America. It was in a little town in Poland, winter, a time of cold and hunger, with which that country had long been acquainted."

I am unaware of the congregation rising.

"Up," says mother.

Up and down. It's one of those quickies of paying respect to the Almighty.

"We were all refugees pouring in from Russia," says Mother. "The synagogues let us sleep there during the night but we had to leave in the daytime during services. The men slept downstairs. Your grandma, my sister and I were in the balcony on the stairs between the seats.

"Twice a day the community cooked us rice soup with canned milk and put a little sweetener in it. That was our daily diet.

"My sister turned her nose up and my mother began to trade our family belongings for tidbits for her. Mother stopped eating so her eldest daughter could have a meal now and then.

"To make matters easier for my mother and sister, I volunteered to do the washing for the town's people, taking bundles of clothes to the river, banging each article of clothing on the ice. We had no rubber gloves then. My hands got so cold they would take an hour to thaw."

I was sympathetic but impatient.

"The lover? You met the lover by the river? You were a siren and sang him to shore."

But it's my mother's story and she will not be rushed.

"I had bad periods, terrible cramps for the rest of

my life," says my mother, "from freezing myself in the river. I paid for my good deed."

"And your sister?"

"She was getting bored. Being poor is very boring.

"'What's to do?' she asked.

"I talked to some young people and, first thing you know, we started a theater. I could give a *drey*, a turn of the head, curtsy, sing, dance a little, memorize lines. And my sister could be ticket-taker. The townspeople joined us and among them was a student, a handsome young man."

"Mama!" I exclaim.

"Slender." My mother is dreamy. "Blond hair, kind eyes, light-blue or hazel, I forget which."

"What happened?" I ask.

The sexton is coming down the aisle. I hurriedly rise for the prayer of meditation.

The sexton can't disturb anyone during this prayer.

"Close call," says my mother.

We are seated again.

My face is buried in the book. The sexton turns around, surveying the rest of the crowd for misbehavior.

"Now!" I tell my mother.

"We play in everything, the young man and I, romance, tragedy, drama, even musical comedy. I'm always in the play with him, but not often as female lead."

This memory is still bitter to her.

"A rich girl in the town would also audition. The people from the village who were involved in our theater would insist that she be the lead, even though they could see that she had a long nose and stringy hair."

"And your sister? Was she finally amused?"

"No, she was jealous. She would help me rehearse and would tell me, 'You talk too soft. You didn't say this right. They'll make fun of you.'"

From the altar the rabbi frowns down at my row. I duck, picking up a glove from the floor.

"And then?" I whisper up from the floor.

"We were getting a little money for acting. Most went to the refugees but a little to the actors. So I said, 'Mamushka, I can't do the washing at the river. I have to rehearse. Send Fanny.'"

"Good for you!" I say.

"My big sister Fanny thought she was the Queen of Sheba. She was born after two miscarriages and my mother was so happy to have her that she bathed Anna in milk. Now, here she was, sticking her hands in ice water in the river."

"She was mad?" I ask.

"You could say that," says mother. "But who noticed? One day a wonderful part came up, Leah, the bride, in S. Ansky's *The Dybbuk*. Leah is the girl possessed by the ghost of the bridegroom betrothed to her in their childhood. Another groom is chosen instead. And the rejected bridegroom dies and haunts her. As expected, the rich girl auditions. Everybody was bowing down before her as usual. But, suddenly, a voice comes out of me, 'I can do both Leah *and* the Dybbuk. You will need only one actress.'"

"I showed them, sweet Leah in love, and then the deep voice of the ghost, the rejected lover, coming out of the mouth of the girl. The rich girl with the long nose pulled her nose even longer, she was so annoyed. And I got the part.

"My friend was in the audience to see me premiere. He was not in this show. There he was, after the performance, front row center, standing and applauding me, and, next thing I know, flowers are in my hand."

"Mama!" I say. I'm thrilled by this tale.

"Then he disappears. I'm performing and he's gone. 'Did you see him?' I asked my sister. 'No,' she said. 'You were throwing yourself at him.' I was so young. What did I know? We all slept in one corner together in the balcony, and I'd wait until my mother and sister fell asleep to cry.

"'Where's your boyfriend tonight?' asked Fanny as she was taking the tickets.

"'He's not my boyfriend,' I said.

"'Then he's got himself another girlfriend,' said Fanny, 'maybe the rich girl with the long nose.'

"The last night of *The Dybbuk*, I took bow after bow, but my heart was heavy. My friend did not come to the final performance.

"Outside of the theater was a woman waiting, a well-dressed, distinguished woman wearing a black hat and veil. The veil covered her eyes.

"'Bronya,' she said my name hesitantly.

"'Yes,' I said, 'I'm Bronya.'

"'Come this way, dear,' she said, 'away from the crowd.'

"I stood still. Why should I go with a stranger?

"'I have something to tell you,' she said in a soft, sad voice.

"Then she told me about my friend who had an accident, a terrible accident."

I'm startled by a hand hitting the pulpit.

"Where is courtesy?" booms the rabbi.

Mother and I pause but not for long. She has to tell and I have to hear the story.

"He was playing tennis and tripped. He hit his head and became unconscious.

"'Can I see him?' I asked his mother.

"'No, my dear. Nobody can ever see him again.'

"We both stood there and cried.

"'He spoke of you to me,' said his mother, 'and made me promise to deliver this to your hand.'

"The woman gave me a little cask with a ring inside of it and then she turned and left the theater."

Another thunder clap on the pulpit.

Mother and I wait for the echo of the hand hitting against wood to fade away.

"Where are they?" I ask out of the side of my mouth. "The cask? The ring? I never saw them."

"They came to a mysterious end," says my mother. "They disappeared."

"In your travels from Poland to America?"

"No," says mother. "In my bed. I hid them under my pillow and one day I put my hand under the pillow and they were gone. I couldn't accuse. The balcony was filled with those of us awaiting our visas. I searched my pillow and covers. I hunted everywhere. I asked everyone, but the ring my friend gave me on his death bed was stolen."

"Did you suspect anyone?" I ask.

"If I did, what could I do about it? I could accuse, make a scene. But I was a good little actress and knew nothing was to be gained. So I acted as if nothing had happened and went on holding my head high. I never shed a tear unless it was on stage. And they never knew how much I cared. I had *that* satisfaction."

"And then, Mama?"

"And then I came to the Golden Land, where I worked in the laundry since doing the laundry seemed to be my specialty. And I went to night class. And met your father. And lived happily ever after."

"Did you, Mama?" I ask. "Really."

"I wasn't Leah for nothing," says my mother.

All week I think of my mother's secret. I blame Aunt Fanny. My anger grows as I build a case against her. I will ask Mama more Friday night.

I arrived and instantly begin talking.

"Did you ever accuse your sister?" I ask my mother, shaking down my umbrella, folding the raincoat wet side in.

"I didn't need to get even," says mother. "Life got even with her. If she expected everyone to bow down to her, if she expected ever again to be bathed in milk, she was sorely disappointed. No husband, no child wants to be a subject of the Queen of Sheba."

She looks at me.

"That's my story. Now you have to keep your end of the bargain," she says.

"What bargain?" I ask.

"You also had a secret, one you kept from me," she says.

The pianist is playing liturgical music to get us in the mood. The rabbi sits meditating with his eyes closed before the service.

"Don't try to make believe," says mother. "You were sixteen, seventeen."

I have no memory of sixteen, seventeen.

"You tell me, if you remember," I say.

"No," says mother, "yours to tell and mine to hear."

"Remind me a little," I say.

Mama jump-starts me. "That first year of college you acted flighty. You were an early admission, too early, if you ask me, for your own good."

"What else happened?" I ask. "Gimme a hand."

"You weren't feeling well," remembers Mama. "You stayed in bed. Then your boyfriend of the time, a track star, if I remember, came over and you were whispering together and telephoning in the front foyer."

"How do you know all this?" I ask.

"A mother knows everything about a marriageable daughter," she says.

I have a sudden memory.

"Is that the time, you came home from the movies. You'd left your key and I let you in the door. First thing, without a hello, nice film, you slap my face," I say.

"I might have," says Mother.

"Why? What was that about?"

"You were in trouble with your athletic boyfriend."

"I don't get you," I say.

"I had just seen *Mildred Pierce* with Joan Crawford and Ann Blyth. The daughter shamed the mother. The mother was good and what did the daughter do in repayment? She seduced her mother's boyfriend."

"Your boyfriend was dead," I remind her, "and you were married to Dad. Why did you slap me? Another time, you saw a movie, and again came home and hit me."

"*Pinky*," says Mama, "with Jeanne Crain. A Black daughter trying to pass for white, snubbing her mother and hurting her mother's feelings."

"What did I have to do with that?" I ask.

"You remember how we get slapped when we begin to bleed?" says Mama. "So the daughter won't disgrace the family. So I slapped you to remind you again."

The singing is sweet, one line repeated, "Let me open my heart to you in truth."

"Tell the truth," says my mother. "What did you do dirty?"

"Thirty years ago?" I ask.

"It doesn't matter when," says my mother.

She turns to me in rage and I believe she is about to hit me again.

156

"Mother," I say, "I'm here because of you, twice a week for eleven months."

"Don't make me feel guilty," says mother, "just because you do your duty."

"Then there's no way to please you," I say.

The pianist begins a series of songs about the arrival of the bride of the Sabbath.

"What was your secret?" asks my mother.

"My secret," I say, "is that I found your cask and ring."

"What are you talking?" asks mother.

The congregants rise to face the doors of the synagogue and the outside world. They welcome in the *callah*, "Come, bride, come."

"You're trying to hurt me," says my mother, "digging up old memories."

"I'm not trying to hurt you," I say. "I'm trying to keep my privacy."

"Nothing is private, even years later," says mother. She narrows her eyes at me. "You, just after your Sweet Sixteen, or seventeenth birthday, had an abortion. Am I right or am I right?"

I am quiet. The congregation faces front again. The rabbi looks up to see who is still buzzing.

"You got pregnant from your letterman and arranged for an abortion," insists my mother. "Tell it. Let it come out."

"I'll never tell you," I say. "It's not your business. You weren't in my bed like your mother and big sister with you. Don't get back at me for them."

"Go home!" says my mother. "Who needs you? A fallen woman prays for me."

I put on my raincoat to leave in the middle of services.

"Wait," says my mother. "I got a little carried away." I will never forgive her.

I sit in my coat and not another word do I say until she softly wishes me a good *Shabbat*, this Sabbath holiday.

I grunt.

"Next week?" asks mother. "Same time, same station?"

I leave her and walk out, mingling with the parishioners.

The rabbi is at the door, shaking hands. He keeps me at his side a moment.

"An ideal daughter," he says. "You know, though, the eleven months is over. Let your mother have a chance at redeeming herself. You could sit down now during the Mourner's Prayer."

I miss Saturday morning services and arrive late the following Friday.

"Hello, stranger," remarks mother.

I turn a cold eye upon her.

"Good to see you," she says hastily.

The hours pass with my barely speaking to her.

"It's getting to my time," she says. "Get up."

I sit stubbornly.

"It's time to pray for me," she says.

I shake my head.

"My months are up," I say. "It's your turn now."

The long introduction to the Mourner's Prayer is read, about continuity and remembering and lessening pain.

"Aw, c'mon," says Mom.

She tugs. Reluctantly I rise. The rabbi is amused. I'm on the job overtime.

I sing the praises of God, the ancient prayer also for scholars. My mother sits satisfied.

"I'm not satisfied, Mother," I say. "You did wrong then and also now."

"Just tell me one thing," whispers Mama.

I don't answer.

"Was I right?"

"You were right, Ma," I say. "I did something wrong."

"I knew it," says mother.

We're at the end of the service. I'm up and out.

"Wait! Wait!" says mother.

The next week, mother can barely contain herself.

I'm still in my coat when mother says, "It was sex that did you in, wasn't it?"

"It had nothing to do with sex," I say.

"What else is there to trap a young girl?" asks mother.

"I was Sweet Sixteen or was it seventeen? There were all those boys. There was all that politics. On every floor of Main Hall was a different political party, Democratic, Republican, Socialist, Communist. I couldn't go by a booth without engaging in discussion. I couldn't pass a stairwell without talking politics. I couldn't have a cup of coffee at the campus hang-out without arguing. I cut a class, then two, then whole days."

"You said you were in the library." My mother is shocked.

"There too, writing notes, whispering, comparing articles. It was a heated time when I was in college."

I am almost smiling. That may have been my education.

"So," says mother, "what happened?"

"Before I knew it, with all the meetings, the Eugene V. Debs Society, the Veterans Against the War, whatever, it was Finals and I hadn't done a damn thing all semester."

"It catches up," says Mother righteously.

"No way to pass. I confided in my friend on the track team. He was a sympathetic boy who tried to keep me from being expelled."

"Expelled!" says my mother. "Who would think from an early achiever?"

"My boyfriend got his doctor cousin to write me an excuse that I had been bedridden with the flu all semester and couldn't study. The cousin stood there in his white coat, holding the note at us with a disgusted look. 'Bedridden, indeed!' he said. My friend and I were so humiliated we could not look at one another again."

"The letterman?" asks mama. "He stopped dating you? Who did he think he was? Just a jock."

I say, "I ended up on probation with a lot of low C's

and a D in German. The letterman went to law school and married the editor of the college newspaper."

"The runner?"

"The runner ran away," I tell her.

"Let him go," says my mother. "You got someone better and didn't have to go running after him."

"I was afraid to tell you what was happening," I say. "You hit me twice for something I didn't do. What would you do to me for something I did?"

"This was different," says my mother.

"So, I hid my transcript from you. I forged your name when the grades were sent home. You didn't have a clue as to what was happening."

"I admit I got it all wrong," says mother. "But a girl on probation isn't a shame to the family. A girl with an abortion is. So, you see, it all turned out."

"No, Mama," I said, "it didn't all turn out."

"Look at you," says my mother. "Good husband. Nice clothes. Full refrigerator. Children grown up. It turned out."

"I turned out less than I could have been," I say. "Stuck where I was, never to transfer, not eligible for scholarship."

"You got a good enough education for a girl," says my mother.

"I was a baby, Mother," I cry. "My future was set when I was just a kid."

The woman ahead of me hears me sniffling and hands back a tissue.

"No one guided me."

"No one guided me either," says my mother.

"But I wanted to be somebody," I say.

I weep again. Another tissue is passed back.

"So did I," says mother. "I wanted to be an actress, but the family voted me down."

"The family?" I ask.

"Two to one," she tells me, "against my going to school in America."

"Your mother and big sister voted against you?"

Mother nods. "Majority wins in a democracy," she says. "And that was the end of a perfect day."

"Yeah," I say, "a perfect day."

"So don't upset yourself, you brought no shame on our name," says mother.

"And no glory, either," say I.

Before we're ready, it's time for the Mourner's Prayer.

"Help me up," says Mom.

She's been shrinking. She holds onto the bench in front of her to keep herself steady.

"So, now you're praying for yourself this twelfth month," I say.

"No," says my mother. "I got unfinished business. I'm praying for you."

"I'm not dead," I tell her.

"You could be a little livelier," says mother. "You could still go back to school, improve yourself. It's not over until it's over."

I stand there stunned. The rabbi shakes his head at me. I sit down and let my mother carry on.

WHISPERING

I WALK ON THE CLIFFS OF LA JOLLA WITH MY mother. My mother and I eavesdrop on the ocean.

"This is something different," says my mother, "walking along in the middle of the day like a lady."

Whispers waft up from the sea to the cliff. The whispers clarify: a breathy laugh, a lullaby, the intrigue of lovers.

My mother's voice has become shyer, softer. She was once a member of a choral group. Before a recital, she would insert earrings into the stretched hole in her ears, apply a touch of cologne. She stood stocky and proud, another rounded mouth in the group. Her wavy, white hair was translucent in the stage lights. When I visit her retirement community to attend services with her, she sings into the prayer book, closing it on her voice.

Mother and I are having an outing together. This is her first night apart from Dad in fifty-eight years.

"How does it feel?" I ask her.

"I'm a bachelor girl," says my mother gaily and takes my arm.

She calls this, "Walking Polish," arm-in-arm.

My mother and I look below at the beach where the tables are being set up for the performers. The waves beat against the sea wall. The ocean slaps the shore of Children's Cove. It's an amphitheater of natural elements. The stage is the beach and the audience will sit in the bleachers, stand on the sea wall or be seated in chairs where the rock has been hewn into alcoves.

"This is your stage set, Mother," I tell her. "And I will be up there watching you."

The production people are setting up speakers next to us. They box the speakers and weight them with sand bags. The discourse of the women will travel from the beach below up to the round, black mouths of these boxes.

"I'm getting nervous," says my mother. "Let's talk over the questions."

Tomorrow the production crew will spread white tablecloths on the tables. Around each table they will place four chairs. On the tablecloth will be a sheet of four questions.

This day will be different from all other days because, on this day, elderly women will be oracles at the sea, speaking in their true range, from deep to high, about matters of import: their aging, preparations for dying, their sense of freedom, how they feel about the women's movement.

Some of these questions, I, as a daughter, could

never ask but I must hear how she speaks of the body in which she dwells. I must know if she thinks of her time as finite.

Mother and I read the sign near the Life Guard Station that is headquarters for the event: "Whisper/The Waves/The Wind: This is a work of art."

My mother is a work of art.

"The events taking place are part of a planned performance. Your cooperation is requested to allow the performance to proceed without interference."

"Who would interfere?" asks my mother.

"A rude sea gull, rain, high winds, surfers, vendors, mothers and babies, transistor radios."

It's a risky business this outdoor performance piece.

"Do you like my white slack suit?" my mother asks. "I dug up an old outfit."

I don't tell her it looks dug up: the blouse is too tight, strangling the neck, pinching the arms, pulled straight across her large bosom. And the pants, polyester across moons of buttocks. But, my mother is my mother. Shopping is a chore for her. New outfits are wasteful. Yet she knows she has to dress in white, like all the others in the great flock with the down-covered heads.

Soon I will watch the parade of white tennis shoes, white Red Cross shoes with heavy arch support, of shiny white plastic shoes, white leather moccasins, the steadier among them on thongs, on heels. One hundred and sixty elderly women, from sixty-two to ninety-nine years of age, will be heading towards the sea.

I think about women and water. Women have always headed to water. At the shore we beat our clothes, washed our bodies, washed our hair—a bed of hair. We would spread the wet hair, separate it, play it like a harp as it dried.

We filled the cooking pots, watered the plants.

And, in our bodies, was a sack of water, a floating sack of water.

This production, the Whisper Project, is the work of Suzanne Lacy. I would ask her how she plans a performance piece with non-professionals, how she controls the elements of this tableau.

"Suzanne said we cannot wear colorful hats," says my mother, "or carry our purses."

She, like all elderly women, worries about her purse. They unwillingly surrender their pocketbooks, the handle on their lives, an attache case of their artifacts: the billfold, compact, comb, hanky, nitroglycerine for angina, lipstick, cologne flask, and, in my mother's bag, 3 × 5 cards with her notes for the questions that will be asked at the shore.

"Someone will guard all the purses," I say.

The waters of the Pacific have become choppy. The sunset is pink, a hint of purple, a swath of cloud. The rock outcroppings are fierce against the soft sky.

"Why this name, Whisper?" mother asks.

Because women are whisperers.

Women whisper not to awaken the children, or to say something comforting into the soft ear. Women whisper in confidence; women whisper in modesty.

I elongate the word: WHISSSPURR. The sound is the word. It makes a soft rustling sound like leaves or the surf. On May 19th, one hundred and sixty women are coming here to the surf and surfacing in full voice.

When did my mother whisper?

"Shh. The neighbors will hear!" she whispered furiously when I developed an adolescent shriek.

Or whispering into our hair if she were proud, whispering if sorry when we hurt ourselves. Sung whispers.

"Loo lee lu
mama nu,
loo lee lu
to you."

My mother and I are sharing a double bed at the motel in La Jolla. The drapes are slightly drawn. My mother's face is lit by the moon. She is a different mother from the mother I knew as a child. She feels different, the feel of her skin is softer; her hair has tamed its curls. Her mouth is open with her breathing. Her teeth have changed. The silver in the cavities has darkened. She has gaps in her mouth. They are not the even white teeth that, until late in life, never needed filling or pulling.

"The dentist never asks me," she told me the first day of my visit, "he just pulls."

Now it's an old fence, pickets missing.

I would place an iron on the time past, smooth out the forehead, color the hair, tighten the chin.

I've had to search for her eyes behind the glint of

glasses, or my Dad's ears under the bulk of hearing aids.

I feel suddenly afraid. I want to awaken her to comfort *me*. I am afraid of losing her. I am afraid of aging.

"Mama," I whisper, "don't leave me. I fear the slackening of youth."

I fear falling. There is an avalanche occurring, a slippage. The calendar is shifting, reckoning time at a reckless speed.

"Mama," I say to her sleeping back, "will all my features slide off my face? Will my chin rest on my chest? Will my eyes become reacquainted with my toes? Will my breasts and belly be one hump?"

My mother snores softly.

"And what will I do about my family? I'm only in the middle of their story."

I rise and move to an arm chair, studying her.

My mother was the young woman of my babyhood, playing snowballs with me. She was the young matron with dark hair parted to the side and large grey eyes. She was the mother, still young and slender, who helped me with her first grand-daughter. All of those mothers cannot be leaving me—heading out to sea.

May 19th dawns, a warm, bright day.

"Let's rehearse on the balcony," says mother.

We have ordered room service and move the tray to the balcony. Mama smiles at the treat of being served.

She has 3 × 5 cards in her hand.

"How do I feel about the Women's Movement?" she reads. And answers. "To tell you the truth, who's to take care of the children if women are liberated, and how will men feel about the women?"

I shake my head.

"It's *my* question," she says. "I'm the actress here."

She reads her notes, "Divorce hurts the children. It's good to express yourself but don't depress the children by getting too liberated."

"Mama," I say irritably, "The Women's Movement has nothing to do with depressing children."

"Pish Posh," says my mother. "Who's lived longer? On to the next question. 'How's your health?' I could complain about my health but who's listening?

"Third question, 'How do you feel about your loss of freedom at this time?' Because I'm old and dependent I think she means. Well, to tell you the truth, I never had freedom, so why is this different?

"Question four, 'What are your preparations for dying?'"

My mother is suddenly enthusiastic.

"Wonderful. I've made wonderful preparations. Everything paid for, caskets, plots, tombstones. You just have to pay the rabbi, a hundred or so, not more. Some are *schnorers* and try to take money out of your hand as we're breathing our last. And the view, Leila, wait until you see the view, top of a hill, overlooking the ocean. Also, not too close to the road where you have traffic in your ear all night long. We did a good job, your Dad and I, working out our funeral. I'm proud of us."

"Mama!" I cry.

"Don't whimper like a baby," she says. "Who's dying, you or me? I should be crying my head off, not you. After all, how many years do we have left, and will we get to see our grandchildren married? Not at the rate they're going. I should take out the hanky, not you."

We get ready for breakfast, mother in her tight blouse and polyester slacks and I with notebook and pen, for I am assigned by a radio production company to write a script of this event. On the program, along with 160 other women, my mother is listed as an actress.

"They spelled my name wrong," she says. "It figures. I am finally performing but under the wrong name."

She forgets the wrong billing as the day's activities begin.

The white-clad women will breakfast at Casa de Manana, a retirement home in La Jolla, facing the sea. The women sit at tables inside the low, Spanish-stucco building with the red clay tile roof. Casa de Manana, House of Tomorrow. I wait to hear my mother and the other women speak of the past, the present or of what is left of the morrow.

"Welcome, all of you," says Suzanne Lacy to the women gathered at the Casa. "You can't see yourselves but you're going to be knockouts!"

Mother blushes. She is girlish, the youngest one at her table of four. Next to her is Suzanne's grandmother, who has permed and blued her hair and sits up proudly during the opening remarks.

On the other side of Mother is a woman with a Viennese accent, who has stretched the directions to wear white into puce. The Viennese hair is in a puff of scarf.

This seatmate says to my mother, "Am I foolish to want to waltz? I love to waltz. Am I foolish, in my eighties, to love to dance to *The Blue Danube*."

"Not at all," my mother assures her.

Suzanne says, "All of us who have worked on this project, women and men, young and old, are doing it for one reason: we all have a mother or grandmother that we feel deeply about, or we wish we did."

Mother is nodding her head. She was an attentive student, those few years she was allowed to go to school.

"We don't know how you feel living this long," continues Suzanne, "how you felt last night, how you hurt, when you felt pleasure, how you felt when loved ones pass on."

My mother is thoughtful. She is remembering. All of the women remember people in their lives. They will talk about those who floated away when they gather at the beach. My mother will think of those for whom she lights the memorial *yahrzeit* candle, at the date of their deaths: her parents, all of her brothers and her sister Fanny, as well as her husband's parents and brother, and a niece and young grand-daughter. The last death was the hardest. Mama's hand trembles when she lights that long-burning candle.

"I want to see all of you elevated to the position of

goddesses," Suzanne ends her remarks, "returned to the oracles you are."

My mother grins. She has spaces missing in her teeth, so it is an impish grin. She will tease me later when I interrupt her. "Shh!" she'll say, finger admonishing, "I'm an oracle."

The street is roped off. The young production people are preparing to act as crutches, guides, walkers, white canes.

In the Casa the women sit with their purses: beaded purses, leather shoulder bags, plastic purses, a plastic blue purse with a brown leather strap. My mother's purse is always too heavy to carry. All of these purses, the cloth bag, the purse with the thin over-the-shoulder strap, the old-fashioned pocket book, will be waiting on their haunches like pets for the return of their owners.

Outdoors, the photographers, the video people are waiting. Some of the still-camera people have names like F. Sharp, Pasha, Jacuzzi.

The women await their instructions, sitting as if at a garden party. Then the oracles, the goddesses shove aside their chairs and prepare for the performance.

The women walk to the rhythm of a tape pre-pre-pared by the sound person, Susan Stone. The women march to the high-pitched calls of gulls and the throat-clearing fog horns. The women march with dignity, single file or in twos, to the beat of the waves. It is as if they were boarding an ark and sailing out to sea. My mother floats among them.

These are the performers I note in my pad:

A Caucasian woman, ninety-nine, at the head of the line, her aluminum walker sparkling in the sun.

Women shy and hesitantly blinking in the brightness of the day.

Women with swollen ankles, heavy stockings.

A Chicana in long white satin-trimmed wedding dress, on crutches.

A Caucasian with a large straw bonnet.

A petite Fillipina in white slack suit with white, small-brimmed hat, a hump on one shoulder, who winks as she goes by.

The woman from Vienna with a puce scarf holding her bun in place, and a needle-point vest in subdued colors.

An African-American with a flowered band around her large hat.

Another woman with a German accent, short blonde hair, white earrings, white crocheted scarf.

A line-up: a Japanese family, mothers and grand-mothers, with jet-black hair.

A tall Caucasian woman in mesh jacket holding the hand of a shorter woman.

Cambodian nuns with shaven heads and white togas.

An African-American with white scarf, white straw hat, white hoops of earrings.

A Caucasian with strands and strands of white beads.

Helmets of hair go by, close fitting, marcelled, frizzed.

My mother passes. She looks surprised at the multitude of townspeople who have gathered.

Mother is speaking to her marching mate, Mrs. Clare Little, the eighty-seven-year-old grandmother of Suzanne Lacy.

"Why are they laughing?" Mother asks Mrs. Little. "Why are they applauding? Now, Mrs. Little, tell me, why are those people crying?"

I cannot hear Mrs. Little's soft reply as the women cross the street to the cliff, one by one disappearing over the edge. They reappear far below walking heavily on the sand. My mother is like a somnambulist, taking slow steps on the unsteady surface, as she walks towards her table and her questions.

One woman is already speaking and gesturing. A black bird sits on the sand close to her table to hear her.

Who would expect to see elderly women taking over the beach? It is customary for the beach to belong to the smoothly oiled body, the bikini, the muscled athlete. It is surrealistic and unexpected to see this multitude of elderly women sitting in this seascape.

Off the cove an instructor is teaching snorkeling. He and his class are like creatures in the lagoon with their faces covered with green snorkels, with their black rubber surfing suits. On Beach A and B of Children's Cove, the women's white hair is like bathing caps. A white gull dazzles the sky. The tableau has the festive air of a summer wedding. The women talking spiritedly are like flowers in heavy blossom, white peony heads nodding.

"When I climbed down the stairs," my mother told me later, "and saw the blue sky meeting the ocean, I thought I had stepped into heaven."

There is my mother at a distance, but my mother is not my mother. She is not cooking. She is not serving. She is smiling, at ease with her peers. How seldom she has been given this opportunity. She gestures theatrically like an actress.

She had told me yesterday on the balcony of the motel:

"I thought I would become an actress. I was acting in Russia and then in Poland for those two years that we waited for our visas. I thought in America I would surely act, but I had to work to help pay back the passage for the six of us which my aunt had borrowed. So I went to work in the laundry. And then I married. Now, sixty-five years later, at the age of eighty-one, I am competing with Hollywood starlets!"

The women speak and look at one another against the expanse of water.

Their voices are amplified by a loud speaker.

I hear a Caucasian warning the others, "Don't stay in bed."

Another voice, "Now, at this time, I want to do what I want to do."

An African-American, with a rose in her hair, seated at my mother's table, says, "The difference between now and when I was younger is that now I'm slower climbing mountains."

They think about aging.

"Younger people must see me and think I'm not long for this world."

"End of the line," says another.

They speak of death.

"Death is coming closer…I wouldn't waste a minute of my life…"

They talk about old-age homes, some dreading, others accepting.

"I like it here in my retirement home," says a Caucasian, "with my books, my TV. I'm preparing to be content."

"I have a question," says the Viennese, addressing my mother. "Do you think, at eighty-four, I'm foolish to still want romance?"

"With those pink cheeks, you have a right," says my mother.

I wonder about the landscape emptying in the losses of their lives. I wonder if, like the gaps in their mouths, the tongue is always poking for that missing tooth, missing friend, lost sister or brother?

I stand there for forty minutes while the women talk together in intimacy and reflection. As the pageant is ending, I hear one person objecting, "But I haven't finished yet."

The women are tenaciously holding onto things. As they rise they grab onto the tablecloth; they lean on the table and get their footing so they can proceed to the bottom of the stairs. Their stories told, the women can depart, ascend those difficult stairs. The young people will pull them up, as the old women pulled the young up in age.

Babies are playing in the sand next to the empty tables.

The women return to the Casa. Awaiting them, besides their handbags, is a gaily-painted, double-decker bus that will take them to St. James Church for luncheon. The women climb aboard laughing from the upper deck. My mother waves from the window. On the roof of the Life Guard Station Suzanne directs the recessional.

I see my mother on the bus sitting next to her new girlfriends, the African-American with the rose in her hair, the rosy-cheeked Viennese, and proud Mrs. Clare Little. They are whispering, confiding.

Susan Stone, the sound person, will work "Whisper" into a radio program. Susan writes to me from her studio in San Francisco about living with those voices:

"Since last Saturday I feel like a thirty-one-year-old soul possessed by eight-one and sixty-five and seventy-two–year-old voices, cajoling, admonishing, teasing and lamenting age and beauty and sex and loss."

I title my script, "Whisper: Above the Timber Line."

"What is there in that uncharted place, where the trees no longer grow and the voices fade?" I ask. "I would know that data from above the timber line."

We are driven back to my parents' retirement community.

"My actress!" Dad greets her.

They embrace. Two days apart in fifty-eight years.

"So what did you learn?" Dad asks.

"I learned I'm as smart as everybody else," says my mother.

She laughs so hard a button pops on her tight blouse.

I am being driven away and look back at them both waving to me. Dad is chilled and goes in, but mother waves until the airport limo is out of sight. I feel as if she were leaving, not I.

I don't want you to go from me, Mama. Even if you give everything away: your wavy hair to me, your hazel eyes to my daughter. I don't want you to go away. Stay. I'll listen closely to your whispers.

She gives me five more years. And eleven months.

This first edition of
Ghost Stories
is published by
Global City Press
New York City

It is designed by
Charles Nix

The text type is
Granjon from Linotype
designed by
George W. Jones
in 1928

Production was managed by
Burton Shulman

The printing is by
Offset Paperback Mfrs., Inc.
Dallas Pennsylvania

ñ